Coming and Going

Harper Moross

iUniverse, Inc.
New York   Bloomington

iUniverse books may be ordered through booksellers or by contacting:

iUniverse
1663 Liberty Drive
Bloomington, IN 47403
www.iuniverse.com
1-800-Authors (1-800-288-4677)

Because of the dynamic nature of the Internet, any Web addresses or
links contained in this book may have changed since publication and may
no longer be valid. The views expressed in this work are solely those of
the author and do not necessarily reflect the views of the publisher, and
the publisher hereby disclaims any responsibility for them.

ISBN: 978-1-4401-8629-5 (sc)
ISBN: 978-1-4401-8630-1 (ebook)

Printed in the United States of America

iUniverse rev. date: 11/13/2009

HARPER (COMING)

"Such a waste!"

I wanted it on your face, so I could get the money shot, but I cum down your throat. I cum before I have time to pull out and snap the photo. *Damn!* I really wanted to cum on your face! I wanted *you* to want it on your face too, and you said you actually *did*—just like an actress in a real porno.

But now it's too late. We can hardly do another take—my recovery time is way too long, and there won't be enough cum the second time around to make for a decent shot anyway. Not to mention that you have to get back to work and close that deal on the Hunters' farm.

It's your fault. You were moving your mouth up and down my shaft way too fast—like some sort of vacuum appliance they sell on late-night TV! It's not *my* fault I lost control. Working the digital camera *and* concentrating on my performance was too much work. I *told* you I'm not that good at multitasking.

As a matter of fact, sometimes I yearn for the simpler, pre-digital, pre-post-modern days—when it was enough to "get lucky" (the very expression seems so quaint, as if having sex were up to Fate instead of being scheduled online). Expectations were so much more manageable then. As an adolescent, I defined "getting lucky" as having a date that held out the possibility of a goodnight kiss if I could muster up the courage.

These days it's not enough to merely exchange bodily fluids—all life is a reality show, and so you have to pretend to be making porn so you can at least post a decent photo on Facebook or Flickr. Yes, alright, I know, the whole setup—the camera, the kitchen counter, the handcuffs, the bondage tape— was my idea. But, see, I didn't really have a coherent plan. I wanted it all at once—to be dominant, to be submissive, to be a porn star, and to be a porn director, and to be watching the show we were starring in. How did I think I could take pictures while I was handcuffed? It's not like I'm really into all this stuff anyway. I'm just an old-fashioned guy with simple fantasies. I only did set it up this way so you wouldn't think I was insufficiently kinky—some horny old loser who just wants a blow job.

How things have changed! I can remember when *Deep Throat* was a scandal and a revelation. *Wow, a woman can actually do that?* Now web sites tell girls how to deep-throat expertly—and all the teenage boys expect they'll do so.

We've cum such a long way, baby!

Truth be told, trying to have porn-quality sex is one thing, but succeeding isn't easy—especially for a man my age. Tell me, just how am I supposed to make it all work—lose control and still be in control of losing control?

And, you know, it doesn't help that you have no confidence in me. It doesn't help that you just shake your head and say:

"What a *fucking* waste."

All of a sudden you remind me of Bozo the Clown, with your overly made-up round face and that frizzy hair looking like you've just been electrocuted.

"Isn't there any on your tongue, even?" I ask, juggling the camera hopefully, trying to find a perfect angle—not easy with handcuffs on.

With a sigh, you stick out your tongue. But all I can see through the viewfinder are a few rotting crowns, several bridges, and a gap in the back where a tooth was recently extracted. You should make an appointment with my dentist—she's such a gorgeous MILF, I don't mind when she puts her sharp tools in my mouth.

"I swallowed it all," you protest. "What else could I do? You were way down my throat, and suddenly you shoot it. Idiot! And what the fuck? Your cum tastes awful. What have you been eating anyway?"

"For lunch I had a hummus and tabouli sandwich and garlic fries."

"Shit. Next time, eat something normal. Like chicken."

It's weird how your voice sounds like it's coming from a vacuum machine.

I wonder, how *can* those guys in the pornos last so long? They've got these hot slutty women expertly tonguing and sucking them—sometimes two or three of them at once!—and then they fuck these willing women for interminable amounts of time (that long, boring, in-and-out pumping; I fast-forward through those parts). It's sad, really, that in the end the only way they can cum is by jerking themselves off into the open mouths and onto the outstretched tongues of their female co-stars. Why is that?

Hell, I would cum in no time if I got a porn star–quality blow job. And even you, Vera, who tries hard but keeps scraping your teeth on my cock, have no trouble getting results. A point just proven.

And that's the first of all the last things that flash through my mind.

PUBLISHER'S NOTE

Harper doesn't know what he's talking about. He doesn't even know who he *is*.

He's just a horny guy with a bunch of failed marriages and a typical case of erectile dysfunction, who is constantly dreaming up all kinds of crazy shit in his head. He's so afraid of real people and real sex that he decides he'd have a heart attack if he ever got an actual blow job.

That's what makes his story—the one we're publishing here—so richly ironic. He's the last guy in the world you'd expect to be in this kind of role. He's an ordinary and frustrated man, a writer of some talent and imagination but little accomplishment, an heir to a nearly worthless fortune, a guy with way too much time on his hands. He has these "adventures." Sure he does! Let's put it kindly and say he's been having a little trouble lately separating fantasy from reality. In reality he's such a chicken shit he'd *never* do any of the stuff he dreams up. Plus, for all his wild talk of antisocial perversion, he's really a loyal family man. Or would be if he had a family. He failed at that too.

His first wife left him for an older guy.

His second wife left him for a younger guy.

His third wife left him for a younger *girl*.

Then, out of desperation, he pretended to be gay and married a guy his age, a former priest. And that guy—scared straight—left him for Harper's second wife.

Maybe that's what made Harper so desperate that he wrote an entire book claiming that he actually acted on one of his fantasies and suffered preposterous consequences.

See, he's got the mind of a fourteen-year-old trapped in the body of a sixty-year-old. And he's under the delusion that his heart is getting stronger all the time. And the even more self-serving delusion that he's the only one on the planet and the whole world's performing for him.

So why are we publishing his book despite all this? Because we think it's an important cultural artifact documenting the massive shifts in social attitudes during Harper's lifetime. Because the best kinds of memoirs are those disguised as fiction, and vice versa.

And because, quite frankly, if you aren't a celebrity author, your book had better have lots of sex in it. Even lots of bad sex might do in a pinch, as here. So enjoy your read, but remember: truth is a relative thing, but sex is usually better left as a fantasy.

VERA

I'm no Bozo the Clown. For one thing, I'm not white, even though I've sometimes passed for white. For another, my hair isn't really that frizzy. True, the "real" (though not original, merely copyright-owning) Bozo recently died, but that doesn't give Harper Moross the right to use that analogy. No fucking way.

I know his screwy game: he pretends he is still married because it makes him safer and more appealing to married women who are seeking revenge on their husbands for cheating. In my case, though, I'm seeking revenge on my husband for something worse than real cheating: always *thinking* about cheating while being extremely and consistently boring.

I suppose officially I'm still married, so I keep the ring on, but this is not really my idea of wedded bliss, or even wedded ennui. It's more like a loop tape of an old *Ozzie and Harriet* season. It's not just that we don't have any sex ever, it's like we're living in a world where people haven't even *discovered* sex yet. I haven't made use of my sorry-ass husband's limp little cock in a long, long time. Hal's big on theories of social contracts but doesn't seem to care much about marital obligations. He's always staying after work fantasizing that some fishnet-stocking-clad post-feminist Goth student will give him a hand job in exchange for an A in his radical psychology class. He's been reading way too many online blogs written by hookers pretending to be brainy coeds. Lying in the conjugal bed, however, he can't take his eyes off the fucking university's Task Force on Maintaining Diversity report (detailing how to get around the public's smack-down of affirmative action while still pretending to be a public university) long enough to even glance at the new Victoria's Secret negligee I'm wearing—solely because an article in *Cosmo* (I read it in the supermarket checkout line, do you think I would actually buy that skanky-posing-as-upscale crap?) recommended so doing as one of "Twenty-Five Ways to Reignite Your Husband's Sagging Sex Drive." I never even got close to the other twenty-four—though I still want to try #22, which I think involves tying him onto his lawn tractor and digging my high heels into his scrotum (or maybe that was a dream I had).

I'm a former Black Panther with a PhD in philosophy, but I sell real estate now. If you're going to sell out, might as well *really* sell out! When I first got my license, twenty years back, I remember having to scrape the "Fuck Authority" bumper sticker off my VW's rear fender. Now, in the current "greatest financial crisis since the Great Depression"—Hal prefers to call it "the long-awaited collapse of capitalism"—I have to work ten times as hard to make the same amount of money I did a few years ago. But I pride myself on the fact that I'm still *selling houses,* unlike all my colleagues who've given up. Two more closings, tomorrow, in fact, making five this week. Just because my commission on these foreclosure specials is barely enough to pay for the gas I use to show the properties to every Harry and Dick (and some dicks that aren't so hairy) doesn't dim my enthusiasm. No siree! Buyer's market or not, this is my new proud measure of success. Never mind the fact that I and the rest of my former radical friends are blithely leaving their children and grandchildren a dying planet. Selling McMansions below market value is a poor substitute for the Revolution, but a gal's gotta do what a gal's gotta do to keep her self-respect in this miserable phony world.

That's also why—for no valid reason other than mindless entertainment, a badly needed boost in confidence, and proof that I'm still desirable—I agreed to meet Harper in one of my ten-months-vacant-price-reduced bungalows and help his addled brain remember what an erection feels like. He's probably been gobbling Viagra like Pop Rocks to gear up for our rendezvous, which consists of this sequence of horror:

1. Him stumbling in the door, half hour late, mumbling something about "orange barrel fatigue."
2. His insistence on the kitchen counter, the handcuffs, etc. etc. Humor the poor boy.
3. Me pulling down his pants, getting his half-erect cock caught in his ridiculously unsexy whitey-tighties.

4. Him grabbing the back of my hair, me yanking his hand away. "What do you think I am, some cheap whore?"

5. My chipped painted nails gently scratching his balls and my mouth closing around the tip of his cock just as my cell phone rings. "Excuse me, I have to get this." "Jesus, can't you *ever* turn that thing off?" "It's my *job*, honey, if you even know what a job is."

6. My cleverly closing the final gap on the sales price for the Plummer place (overly kitsch Victorian retro rehab with undisclosed soggy basement) while keeping him erect with flicking fingers and occasional darting tongue. "What the hell?" he complains. I hang up. "What? I thought you *liked* phone sex."

7. Seeming hours pass, though it's probably just minutes. My jaws ache.

8. He fuckin' cums in my mouth. Without warning. Like a snake upchucking a pig. Big, sticky, stinky gobs. Especially annoying because I had to go through this entire rigmarole of acting like I *wanted* to be forced to beg him to cum on my face, which is what a good little slut deserves for being such a fucking little tease, blah blah blah, when in truth I would prefer he cum anywhere on me—face, hair, sagging tits, hell my fucking elbows for all I care—anywhere *except* in my mouth, because I *hate* the taste of cum, especially

his foul-smelling chick-pea-flavored cum, and I can't exactly *spit it out* on my client's newly stained hardwood floor, especially after convincing the desperate sellers to pay $1,800 to get my buddies to strip it, of which I get my customary $600 kickback. Plus, I have to keep pretending I actually not only *want* it on my face, but that I want him to take a photo of me with it on my face, so that it resembles the pornos he's constantly watching. That's why I brought my digital camera, which, idiot that he is, he can't even figure out how to use properly. Thus my succinct summary judgment: "What a waste." Indeed. Guy is *how old* and he hasn't even learned the self-control of a high schooler?

9. Then, to top it off, his eyes fucking roll back in their sockets. How the fuck am I going to explain this when my lipstick is all over his cock? Quickly I unclasp the handcuffs from his wrists. His body feels soggy and sweaty. Oh God! *I was just showing him the Jenn-Air …*

HARPER

I'm not at all sure you exist.

For the sake of convention, I'm *pretending* to believe that you, dear "reader," are one of six-point-something billion other "people" who live on this "planet." That's how the game is played. I am a "writer" so I "write" things and they get "published," and supposedly some number of faceless "readers" "read" those things I "write."

Right.

For nearly six decades, I've accepted the "reality" of living in an insulated cocoon amid a world of unspeakable violence. But it all seems increasingly implausible to me. Of late I've become more satisfied with an alternative explanation: that you don't exist, and that I'm the subject of some preposterously massive mind control experiment to discover how much brutality a human can tolerate hearing about—but never directly experiencing and being absolutely powerless to stop. A lifetime spent inundated with reports of people brutalizing and being brutalized while I continue to live in a bubble of boredom. An unending snuff movie playing in the background of a comfortable, "normal" American life.

I can no longer stand the fact that I can stand this world.

I am me and you are he and you are me and we are all together? Oh, sure. For a moment I believed that. But now I'm not even sure there *is* a you. And if we're all together, how come most of you are starving and mutilated and living in fear—and I'm untouched?

The official, for-publication story goes like this: Harper Sebastian Moross is born into blissful parochial suburban ignorance in the middle of the night in the middle of the summer in the middle of the century in the middle of a hospital room in the middle of the country in the middle of a noisy thunderstorm.

The heart is beating. It has no desire other than to beat a few billion times. But the mind will give it plenty of more complicated desires in due time.

Just about everything important that little Harper is told turns out to be a fucking lie.

Like:

Why did God make you? God made me to know him, to love him, and to serve him in this world…

And:

…indivisible, with liberty and justice for all.

And:

…the victim of a lone gunman.

And:

Crest has been shown to be an effective, decay-preventing dentifrice that can be of significant value when used in a conscientiously applied program of oral hygiene and regular professional care.

I got the cavities to prove this wrong. Not just the ones in my teeth, but the ones in my soul, forming the void where naïve faith used to be.

See, once upon a time I and my siblings tried to believe that everything on TV was true, and so we imitated the families we saw there, like the Cleavers and the Nelsons. In the future we would live like the Jetsons. In the past we lived like the Flinstones.

June and Ward, Ozzie and Harriet, and my parents didn't ever talk about the things that immediately predated these shiny, happy times. No one's parents ever did.

Eat your Maypo and ignore what you read in books: that my birth was preceded by thirty years of massive insanity and carnage that everyone seems to be pretending *didn't just happen a few years ago.*

First, a *war to end all wars* in which millions of men spent years stuck in holes in the mud and slaughtered each other day after day, to advance to new holes in the mud a few yards east or west. To live month after month in ditches like vermin and then die like dogs, cut down by the men in other ditches, who are just like them except for wearing different colored uniforms. Death toll: *nineteen million human beings.* And nobody can even say for sure what that war was all about— something about an archduke?

Then, the Great Depression, which didn't seem all that great—what with millions of people eating dust and soup and not much else.

Then five years of utter mayhem known in rather understated terms as "World War II." Five years of unending horrific terror. *Death toll: forty-eight million human beings.*

Growing up in the house by the lake, I often ride my bike up and down the driveway and across the front yard from tree to tree. I make the paths into imaginary roads, pilfering the quaint names from the countryside around my grandmother's house in Maryland: Rolling Road. Tobacco Pike. I can even smell the honeysuckle in my imaginary world.

The world seems fresh, green, and blooming. When I study maps—I love to do that—I keep discovering so many interesting place names: Walla Walla. Okefenokee. Addis Ababa. Uruguay. Irkutsk. Ulan Bator. Kalamazoo. Hamtramck.

Fascinating, that there is this world already mapped out, a world that existed before I was born, plotted and divided into countries and cities and towns, so many of them, with so many names. It all seems so orderly, so wholesome.

But it barely conceals the recent chaos. How did the spring rains and the winter snows so quickly wipe out the stench of all those millions of corpses? Dresden. Iwo Jima. Normandy. Ukraine. Hiroshima. Nagasaki.

History says it all happened. Just a few years before I was born, my nation's government vaporized two cities. Serves 'em right, so the story goes, for being *Japs,* for daring to be born and live in cities controlled by an Emperor who allied himself with a master madman with a ridiculous mustache who incinerated six million people for the unforgivable crime of—of what exactly?

Practicing a different religion, even the ones who weren't religious, or being of a different race, sort of, even though they'd been living together for centuries with their persecutors and couldn't reliably be told apart.

Many, many others died, the books said: millions of Russians in the snow, soldiers from many nations in the African desert, Americans and Asians on specks of rock in the Pacific, countless innocents blasted by firebombs that fell from the sky onto their cities. And then—a breakthrough in human history, a quantum leap in killing efficiency—the compression of the laborious techniques of mass state-sponsored murder into an instant. What took Hitler so many years, so many subordinates, and so many guns and ovens to accomplish, our government found a way to do more efficiently—kill massively and indiscriminately in a matter of seconds, without warning, namelessly and wordlessly.

Bones and hearts. Babies suckling at mother's breasts. Young lovers kissing. Fathers walking to work. Fleshy legs and arms and faces. All vaporized in an instant by a weapon created by the same sorts of creatures still living on the same planet with me and now portraying their nature as being accurately represented by comic and utterly harmless TV families.

Flesh, skin, muscle, bones—just like mine.

Trust and love *your fellow man?* How do you feel safe being born into a race of creatures with minds that could not just conceive but execute those heinous acts? Living in a nation that not only is ruled by madmen who could order such acts but is populated by a citizenry that applauds them for doing so? Answer: Watch a lot of TV. Play a lot of cards. And suck your thumb for comfort. Endure all the scolding you get for it but never stop sucking—into first, second, even third grade.

If you never acknowledge what happened and pretend it could never happen again, you might enjoy an illusion of safety. By the time I was born, all that hatred, anger, and lunacy were over and done with— that's the story anyway. Another *war to end all wars* has ended, and peace and prosperity are at hand. We are all friends again, those of us lucky enough to survive and live normal—*normal!*--lives.

In *nuclear* families.

The next war will kill everyone on the planet. Life as lived by the Beaver and all the watchers of the Beaver's mundane adventures is an absurd respite of unknowable duration. The Bomb renders every moment on earth precarious.

To grow up under the constant threat of annihilation requires a mental duplicity—either deliberately pretend to forget, or act like it's all fine though knowing you're lying to yourself. Go off to school with a peanut-butter-and-jelly sandwich and apple inside your Hopalong Cassidy lunchbox and stare out the windows all morning watching for the planes to come and drop the bombs (the official name for that week: the "Cuban missile crisis").

By itself the Bomb—meaning, now, tens of thousands of nuclear weapons—overrides all capacity for believing in good, renders ridiculous all sermons and sentiment, makes a ghastly joke out of being alive.

Not to mention all the rest of the ensuing insanity. Chemical and other diabolical weapons. Ethnic cleansing—the very term repulsively antiseptic. Coups and assassinations and cold wars and hot wars. But, like all the other violence that I constantly hear about—car bombing in Baghdad Somalia Madrid Khartoum Beirut Tirkut Kabul Derry— *but which never has touched me personally,* it must somehow be taken for granted.

Has there ever been a more bizarre thing than to be alive in my lifetime? To keep hearing and reading about other people being blown to bits—nameless faceless folks in other countries, yes, but still human beings just like me—and to learn to accept that as part of the background noise of life, like birds singing in the trees? No other generation has ever known about so many people killing other people.

Numbness. Or fear. Or faking the bliss of the ignorant. Those seem to be the rational choices (addiction or going crazy are also options). Fear is always a welcome resort. On TV are all the ads that tell you to be very afraid of all the ways you might die (except not by nuclear annihilation, war, or rising oceans—because none of those risks can be treated with profitable medications). Stroke. Cancer. And, most terrifying of all, *heart attack.* How, I wonder, can the heart *attack* and annihilate its host? How can the heart turn on itself? Isn't its nature always to expand, always to open up wider and love more?

It's said that people can die of a broken heart, of love thwarted and rejected. But it seems to me people are more likely to die of a closed heart—one that never risks anything.

But that's just the sort of thinking that gets me into trouble.

Eventually this becomes starkly clear:
Everybody else dies, but I never do.
So I figure, since there's no other rational explanation for this world I live in, this must be all an experiment. Or maybe a joke. Some sort of weird setup.
I'm still waiting for the punch line. It never comes.

I open my eyes and see a clock floating in white nothingness, like a ghost ship emerging suddenly out of dense fog. But I have no distance perspective. I seem to be floating too, dreamlike, disembodied, somewhere indefinable. The clock is my only point of reference.
Its long spindly black hand and its short stubbier hand point out the time: 7:25. The hands look like those of an umpire signaling *safe*. But I sure don't feel safe.
The numbers are rigid, unyielding. They stand against a backdrop that seems ineffable, deep, an inscrutable, huge white face.
The face of what? Where?

HAL

REPRESSIVE DESUBLIMATION

Professor Pasten (that would be me, but I like the pretentiousness of writing about myself in the third person) writes the words on the whiteboard. He shakes his head as he does. (Even after all these years I can't get used to using markers. I miss blackboard and chalk, especially the smell when clouds of it gush from erasers smacked together.)

His skinny ass sits in his thrift-store slacks like a saggy peach in a produce bin. The girl in the third row from the front, the one with the hair like a thunderstorm, pink lipstick, a face betraying an intricate, indeterminate (and thus currently fashionable) mixed-race composite, and the outrageous outfit—red Keds, white-and-pink striped knee socks, orange fishnets, a green miniskirt, and a midriff-baring teeny white top barely covered by a black mesh thingy and hugged by a short blue-jean jacket—stares at my skinny white ass and bites her lip.

"Can anyone tell me what this means?"

I start to turn around from the board toward the class. Even though I know what will meet my eyes— the faces downturned to laptops or cell phones, IM'ing or texting furiously; the gum-chewing vacant stares into space; the few eager-beavers looking for a sign, a thought, a way to please and get an A; the heads on the desks, sleeping off a hangover—I still allow myself a second of delicious old-school fantasy that what I'll find is a sea of bright, attentive faces, shining with an eagerness to learn, with excitement about challenging assumptions.

One hand goes up. Her: the chubby Korean girl with coke-bottle glasses and the annoying lisp.

"Amy, as always, has an answer ready," I say drolly, feigning great boredom. "Does anyone else care to participate?"

I know I'm supposed to crack wise now, but I've grown very weary of the way the professorial role has morphed into that of standup comic, so I fall back on the familiar sardonic declension.

The professor glances down at the girl with the storm-tossed hair, who seems to be doing something with her hands in her lap.

Shit. What's her name again?

Her eyes glance up and meet mine, glaring. I quickly avert my gaze. I can't be caught staring at the class slut in front of everyone, even though I've gotten a hint from her first paper that she might be the brightest bulb in the room.

She suddenly shoots her hand up, just as she loudly pops a gigantic piece of bubblegum.

"Yes… um…," I point to her lamely.

"Xix," she shouts out. "Why can't you remember my name? It ain't that hard. Only three letters: X. I. X."

Scattered giggles and snorts from around the room, emitted by the few sentient beings paying any attention. For a second the chirps drown out the constant clicking of keys.

"Of course, Miss Xix." I feign nonchalance.

"I ain't *Miss* Anything," she snaps. "Just Xix. I don't like gender ghettoizing." Then her mouth allows a smirk. She seems to be missing one of her front teeth—or maybe it's just colored in with black marker, very likely the latest post-punk thing?

"Go ahead, Xix. Tell us about repressive desublimation." I let out an exaggerated exasperated sigh, the much-put-upon pose that some students occasionally respond to.

Scattered snickers with occasional gusts of air-conditioning-blown Altoids.

"Herbert Marcuse," she says, loudly. "Post-Freudian visionary. Saw the future like it was right inside his eyeballs."

The professor strolls over to get a little closer to Xix. A lanky guy even if slightly stooped by age, on the edge of the lecture stage he towers above her like a lighthouse over rocky shoals.

"That's right. Marcuse coined the term. So why is it visionary?"

"You asking me?" sasses Xix. "Look around. Eighty percent of the kids in here are cybering or sexting as we speak. Half the guys have hard-ons, and most of the girls have wet panties."

At this, there is a slight diminishing of keyboard clatter as a few kids look up from their coding and nudge each other or whisper.

"And how does this activity qualify as repressive desublimation?"

"Hey," says Xix, laughing. "You tell me. You're the teach. But seems to me as long as we're up to our elbows in constant masturbation, it's pretty hard to get your mind out of your own asshole long enough to do any fucking thing to stop the planet from burning up or blowing up, whichever is gonna happen first. So, one of them for sure is."

Immediately her head sinks, and she goes back to whatever she's doing in her lap. Murmurs alternate with roars of approval, squeals of laughter, and one loud fart.

"Actually, fellow explorers," says the Professor, trying to wax coolly ingratiating. "Xix here has nailed it." Then I shift into lecture mode.

"Herbert Marcuse was one of Freud's disciples, but he broke away from his mentor. In the 1950s he could see that increased leisure time and the twin distractions of TV entertainment and advertising might pose a threat to the hegemony of capitalism.

"In *Civilization and Its Discontents* Freud showed how sublimation of libido—libido being the product of the undisciplined id, the childlike, pleasure-seeking portion of the unconscious mind—was necessary for civilization. Repressed libido is sublimated from sexual outlets to artistic, cultural, and commercial pursuits. Thus, according to Freud, civilization runs on rechanneled sexual energy.

"Marcuse wondered how the threat of unleashed libido might impact the hegemony of civilization's institutions."

The sleepers have their heads down again, and the texters are very busy with their fingers. I'm staring at my lectern, aware that my voice is droning. I picture myself as a ventriloquist's dummy.

"Referencing Marx, Marcuse realized that commodity fetishism—the substitution of materialism and money for genuine human relations—could be harnessed by advertisers smart enough to tie their product to libidinal desires, putting commercial materials between the itch and the scratch.

"Thus did market imperatives hitch a ride on sexual liberation. What followed was massive cooptation of social rebellion expressed as cultural change. Threatening stars were turned into safe commodities. It started with Elvis, and continued a generation later with Madonna...."

Why can't I shut the fuck up?

When I stop my monologue, the only ones paying attention are Amy and Stephen, her doppelganger teacher's pet. Everyone else is long gone. I risk a glance at the combustible Xix. She appears to be doing her nails.

I call for a break and leave for the bathroom, thoroughly disheartened.

When the professor returns there is a wrapped-up piece of paper on his podium.

He picks it up, and something falls out—something narrow and plastic and gray, with a button. When he presses the button, a green light atop it goes on.

He thinks he hears a low moan from the front row.

On the paper is scrawled a note in large, perhaps satirically flowery script:

Dear Professor,

Care to test Marcuse's theory?
I am wearing a butterfly vibe.
This remote controls it.
Please, sir, teach me a real lesson.

X.

I quickly press the button off and look around in a panic, making sure no one has seen me picking up the note and the *thing*. As usual, no one is paying any attention. Half the students are still out of the room. The others are pecking away, snoozing, or jabbering. Xix is in her seat, nonchalantly typing on her laptop.

On her laptop a video is playing, with the sound turned down. It's one of her favorites: a girl on a rooftop being fucked by a machine.

How do I know this? She told me, later.

OFFICER H.M. SEBASTIAN

It's been another busy but boring day. Two drunk driving accidents, three PPO violations, and an old woman walking naked down a country road, demented. Turns out she'd escaped from the Evangelical Home.

For this I spent two years of night classes getting a master's degree in criminal justice?

As I walk into the interrogation room, I glance at the TV monitor:

RUSSIAN TROOPS BOGGED DOWN IN GEORGIA

Officer H.M. Sebastian aka yours truly, your humble narrator, sighs. I console myself by thinking of the 500-page draft of my novel. It's ready to send off to agents and publishers, and I'm looking forward to giving it one last proofreading tonight after work. I've finally nailed it. The scene where the stripper does the dance that mesmerizes the entire world just as the solar flare sets off an Electromagnetic Pulse—if I say so myself, it's a brilliant dissection of how we're all distracted by the salacious seduction of scantily clad sirens. It's going to be a sure best-seller, and then I can stop being a police inspector and be a real writer, finally. A *real* writer: H.M. Sebastian. Someone people *notice*.

This job is certainly not challenging my magnificent brain.

The woman is older than I thought she'd be. Pathetic really, not the kind you'd think would be doing this kind of sport. Disgusting—people reverting to their animal natures. She looks distraught, her eyes frantically searching my face for any sign of compassion, for some relief. As always. I used to feel a surge of domineering power at this point. Now, nothing. Nothing at all. The fact that I'm in charge is no more arousing than the time on the clock on the wall: 7:25.

"Just some routine questions, ma'am. No need to be concerned."

I sit down across from her.

"Then why have I been waiting for two hours?"

"Busy place, ma'am. And we don't control the extent of criminal activity on any given day."

I keep my tone deliberately haughty. Officer H.M. Sebastian is the much-put-upon public servant, doing a thankless job.

Her tone is begrudgingly pleading.

"I don't know why I got hauled in here. Can't you cut me some slack?"

I sigh audibly.

"You're here because you were found in a house belonging to someone else with a naked man who wasn't breathing, whose testicles were wrapped in black tape and whose wrists had been handcuffed. We found the cuffs in the trash out back, and your fingerprints are all over them."

The woman sighs and shifts her weight in the plastic chair. I can see that she once must have been quite attractive, but clearly she hasn't been keeping up with her exercise regime lately.

"I already explained that to the other officers several times. I'm the Realtor for the Chases, the owners of the house."

"And what was this man—this Harper Moross—doing there?"

"I was showing him the house."

"And what was he showing you exactly?"

"Look, please...*sir*," she says the last word as if choking it out, like it had to get around a century-old gob of pride stuck in her throat. "My business depends solely on my reputation. If you could just overlook the circumstances..."

"Hard to overlook a naked body."

"Is he dead?"

"I'm not privy to that information, ma'am. I haven't had time to go to the hospital. All I know is that the report says he was not breathing when the medics arrived. His heart had stopped. And, interestingly, his penis was still tumescent."

VERA

I look at the corner of the ceiling and see the security camera. I wince and lean forward across the table. This man is ramrod stiff, typical petty white guy in authority who seems to have a stick up his ass—and about as appealing as a robot, but still…here goes nothing.

"Please, sir, if there's a way we could just forget about his nakedness and the…um…electrical tape. Strike it from the report or something. Please, I'd…I'd do *anything* for you if you would do that."

He looks up briefly from his clipboard, into my eyes, then quickly glances back down.

"Anything? Really now?"

"Yes, sir." My voice is a husky whisper.

"Including what you did for Harper Moross?"

I cough.

"Whatever I need to do, sir."

The man grins like the Cheshire Cat.

"Is that the reason you're such a successful Realtor, Mrs. McNamara?" A triumphant tone now. "You're willing to do whatever it takes to close a deal, aren't you?"

"I'm not *Mrs.* McNamara. I'm *Ms.* McNamara."

I once believed we would start a revolution that would end all wars and bring justice to the oppressed peoples of the world. Now I stare down at my tattered, chipped black heels and try to comprehend how I got here, in this cell, degrading myself to this man, to The Man, and all because of Harper Moross's pathetic little cock.

HAL

I stumble in the front door, head in a cloud. The last few hours are a blur. The thunderstorm moving across my bare chest...her crooked teeth grinning like an idiot...her black lipstick writing "Marcuse" on my belly. I'd lost track of time, completely. Now it's almost dark. I'll have to come up with an excuse. But my brain is too befuddled to do anything but laugh. How did she know where to get absinthe? Where did she learn those knots?

I'm glad Vera is nowhere to be found. I don't have to dream up a story that she won't believe anyway. But where *is* she? It isn't her bridge night.

I turn on the TV and see a man with a head of cartoonishly bushy red hair standing in front of the police station.

"Seb Harpo reporting. Fox 2 News has learned that a real estate agent is being held for questioning in the investigation of the possible death of an heir to a pickle fortune. We're told by sources close to the investigation that Harper Moross, son of Little Mack Moross, founder of the Seven Mile Pickle Corporation, maker of Splvastic Pickles, suffered a heart attack while having an illicit sexual liaison with the Realtor, Vera McNamara, a 59-year-old former 1960s radical who was once investigated in connection with a Weather Underground plot to blow up Selfridge Air Force Base."

What the hell? I reach in my pocket to grab my cell phone, but it's gone. So is my wallet. *What the hell?*

HARPER

Little Harper returns to his pew after taking Communion. Pretending to kneel and bow his head in prayer, he keeps sneaking glances up the aisle. Here come the girls in his class back from the altar, devoutly folding their hands in a virginal steeple while they try hard not to pierce the body of Christ with their tongues but let Him melt in their mouths. Harper checks out their legs. Suzy Villeaux is *not* wearing her dark blue uniform knee socks. She is wearing flesh-colored *nylon stockings*. Harper's cock jumps a little in his pants. He thinks Suzy notices him glancing at her, and he quickly averts his gaze. He looks up to see Mary Miles, with legs so long—she too has nylons on!

After school that afternoon, he goes to his bedroom, locks his door, and pulls out his notebook. Folded carefully inside is the Nylon Chart. With today's results Suzy Villeaux has taken the lead with eighteen days so far this school year, one more than Claudia McManus—

eighteen days of defiance of authority, eighteen days of teasing his desire. A desire he will never act on.

Catholicism is good for stoking defiance.

Here's what Catholicism taught me when I was little Harper:

If you have a sinful thought and you do not let it pass through your mind but hold onto it, it is just as much a sin as actually committing the corresponding sinful deed. This seems to me to be a license to kill, rape, steal, plunder, masturbate, and commit other mortal sins, because if you are already going to hell just for *thinking* about doing these things, why not go ahead and do them—well, at least the masturbating?

The tricky part is trying to determine how many seconds you can legally hold a thought before it becomes a sin. The nuns speak sternly about letting thoughts pass through your mind, but they never give a specific duration. So I experiment. I think about Suzy Villeaux's nylons for one, two, five seconds—not struck down by lightning yet!—then ten seconds, and then…well, eventually I am holding more than just the thought.

Another great thing about being a Catholic, which almost balances out having to go to Mass every day, is that if you confess your sins and do your penance—which is never anything more difficult than mumbling the same prayers over and over again—then all your sins up to that point are erased from your slate. So, even if you are Hitler, if you confess before you die and are sincerely repentant, you can go to heaven. A priest can absolve you of all your sins, right up to your last breath. (However, if you are a baby and die before you are baptized, you will spend infinity in *limbo*. Hitler ends up in heaven, but innocent newborn baby denied entrance. I guess that's what they mean by "God works in mysterious ways!")

And here's the really great part: Even if there isn't time to find a priest to absolve you of your sins as you are dying, if you are contrite and confess *in your mind,* you will still be forgiven. I see a big loophole here. For most of my childhood I am terribly afraid I will die at any moment, like my mother or the people of Hiroshima or Nagasaki—or like everyone in the world if the Soviets launch their ICBMs. That's why I keep a constant lookout for impending doom. Every time there's a thunderstorm, I cower in fear of being struck by lightning or being swept away in a tornado like Dorothy. Because I have been entertaining *impure thoughts* about nylon stockings for more than five seconds, I must repent before I die or I will spend eternity in hell. So whenever a storm comes up I mumble to God how sorry I am for charting nylons, and I promise to go to confession at the next opportunity, knowing full well that I won't actually go to confession when the storm subsides and tomorrow morning I will go to Mass and look for more rebellious legs in nylons.

Soon it seems to me, pubescent Harper, that God is a fool who can be taken in rather easily. He is a dupe, disabled by the conflict between his nasty habit of always watching your thoughts and his overwhelming desire to be infinitely merciful.

Supposedly this same God is all-powerful, yet he sent his son to earth so some stupid human beings could kill him. And his son died for our sins, yours and mine, even though we wouldn't be committing those sins for another two thousand years, but that is why we can sin like crazy and be forgiven, because God's son suffered in our place, so we don't have to. And his crucifixion made people feel guilty enough about being human and sinful that they go to church by the millions, twenty centuries later, and mumble those prayers over and over—not a bad deal, really, if that's all it takes to be allowed to continue to be sinful.

If you believe in "history," millions of people have been killed in the name of religion, and on it goes, wars without end, amen. And has any religion had more people killed in its name than Catholicism? But at least the Catholics are marginally more honest about being part of the bloodthirsty human race. After all, Jesus is a promoter of cannibalism—he wants you to eat his body and drink his blood!

However, if you're not a Catholic and you don't believe the bread and wine are actually the body and blood of Christ, and you haven't gone to confession, you won't be allowed to swallow a piece of God's flesh and wash it down with a little blood—because you are quite obviously a heathen!

Be that as it may, no one is going to eat me after I die. Just right before, apparently. Compared to Jesus, maybe that's not such a bad deal.

FOX 2 NEWS

"How did you get this story so fast?"

Ever the smug dominatrix, Mackenzie Krieg has an expression on her face that the Reporter has never seen before—a variation on her usual sadism that allows, at the grim corners of her mouth, the escape of a barely detectable drop of begrudging admiration.

"I have my sources." The lanky redheaded Reporter towers above the small sparkplug boss who hates his casual, slovenly work clothes. She always wears dark power suits to armor her big-assed body.

On the TV monitor above her desk he notices the news crawl at the bottom. FORTY DEAD IN BAGHDAD SUICIDE BOMBING...BRITTANY SPEARS DENIES HAVING PLASTIC SURGERY...NEW CLASHES IN SOUTH OSSETIA...

"All you do is sit in front of your laptop all day," she sneers.

"Like I said. My sources."

"Well, we got lots of response to your piece. What can you give me for a follow-up tomorrow?"

"What I usually give you," grins the Reporter. "Just what you want. More salacious scandal."

She reaches out her hand as if she is about to slap him, then retracts it.

"I don't want vanilla, Harpo," she says, her voice hard as marble. "I want something that's gonna make little old ladies in Madison Heights cum in their Depends."

"Yes ma'am!" he smiles. "You'll get that—and more. I promise."

VERA

I walk out the door of the police station into a buzzard's nest of bastards with cameras and microphones and notepads. I try to shield my face with my arms.

"How did you kill him?"

"Did you bite off his cock?"

"Why were you meeting him?"

"Why did you broadcast it?"

I push through the crowd and start to run. A reporter grabs my arm. I'm spun around, and there's Hal, right in front of me. I look away in shame.

But Hal, dear Hal, holds out his arms, and I rush into them. I start to cry.

"Do you know what's going on?"

"I saw it on TV," he says.

"How does everyone know about this?"

"I have no idea."

HARPER

The clock.

No longer on the wall. In the town square, clanging menacingly, in *Wild Strawberries*. In the desert, going limp—Dali's.

Limp, like *my* cock was far too often when trying to impress.

Clock. It's just a cock with another cock—that big, stiff "L"— inserted between the open C and the big O. Cock between cunt and orgasm?

My stream of consciousness always is a trickle heading down a gutter.

A familiar groove.

Between glimpses of the clock, I fall into a deep slumber. I dream of presidents. I once memorized all of them, in preparation for a tryout for *Jeopardy*. I never made it to the tryout, though, because that was the day Daddy died, amazingly not from his constant drinking, but from a suitcase that fell out of the plane that was carrying Alex Trebek back home to Canada. Ever since then, I've blamed past presidents for my sinful thoughts.

Like the time Taft decided to explore his underexploited submissive side. Tired of being a straight-laced Republican, he agrees to the demands of a sensual dominatrix—but comes to regret it.

TAFT

On a winter Saturday afternoon, Taft encounters Michelle in the Dead Presidents chat room. She says she's married and her husband encourages her extracurricular domming—but it is hard to explain to the children why Mommy sometimes dresses up in a strange outfit and leaves the house at night. Now her husband's taken the kids on an errand—they'll be back in twenty minutes.

She demands Taft go on cam. He spends a few minutes fumbling with the thing. He isn't used to having to work stuff by himself. The webcam appeared in his office one recent day, no doubt sent by his political opponents to entrap him. He doesn't care. He is sick to death of presidential protocol and choking from the cigar smoke in the Capitol cloakroom, making deals with the sycophants and the slime-balls. He gives Michelle his private phone line.

"Get a ruler." Those are her first words. Did she *know* who he was? What if the length of his cock were to end up being published in the *Washington Post*? Still, he complies. He likes games, and the being-president thing is getting old anyway.

He grabs the ruler and holds it up in front of the cam. It's green and wooden.

"Slap your cock with the ruler."

Not for measuring? Stop the presses!

Tentatively he slaps it against his already-erect cock, and the impact makes it sway a little, like a palm tree in a slight breeze.

"Again. Harder."

Again. Harder.

It stings. Being a wimp, Taft winces and cries a little. That's just what she is after—an admission of vulnerability. Suddenly he thinks: this is a lot like an election campaign. Nothing but constant degradation. He's used to that.

"Harder." Her voice is stern, and the words are sounding more clipped and truncated. More authoritarian and less forgiving.

His brain buzzes, like a fly is trapped in there. He is *very* aroused—a woman he doesn't know is ordering him to do things with his cock, and there's a rush of risk: the very real potential of ruining his career and sending him back to Ohio to spend his life in permanent disrepute and fly fishing.

Yet he doesn't like how much it hurts.

"Do you have any rubber bands?"

Now a dozen flies are dancing inside his head.

"Yes."

He fumbles around in his desk drawer and finds a large red one.

"Put it around your cock."

No time to waste. Any minute her little darlings or his Chief of Staff might come running through the door.

He ties it around, one loop.

"Another one. Tighter."

He grabs another and loops it once, then twice. That's not easy, given how hard he is, and he's squeezed mightily.

"Keep going. Another one."

The third increases his alarm as his cock partially disappears behind the constricting bands.

"I don't have any more," he lies.

"Slap it with the ruler. Hard."

Now the problem is finding a place to slap. The head is the only surface left uncovered. But it's the most excruciating landing spot.

"Keep slapping." Her voice sounds a little breathless. His brain is on fire with fear. What if this were to cause a permanent injury—what would the First Lady say if she discovered it during a session of congress? His besieged cock is looking a lot skinnier by the minute.

He is participating in his own torture.

"Now beg me for what you want."

Taft laughs, nervously.

"What I want about what?"

Michelle is angry.

"Why are you laughing? Do you think this is funny?"

Does Taft think it is funny that he is sitting in his office, his pants around his ankles, broadcasting an image of his cock over this system of fiber optic cables and ether connections (invisible things in the air?) and whatever else (he couldn't comprehend what) constituted this technology, and a woman he has never met or talked to before this afternoon has made him tie up his cock with three rubber bands and slap it with a ruler, and that he might be permanently injuring the most precious part of his anatomy and ending his presidential term prematurely because he is foolish enough to trust this anonymous woman isn't a sadistic torturer, when there is absolutely no reason to trust that she has his welfare in any part of her malevolent, selfish mind—and that now there is a serious semantic problem?

Not funny exactly. Ludicrous.

"I don't know what you want me to beg for."

She sounds disgusted.

"Obviously, I want you to beg for me to let you cum."

"But to be honest, I don't want to cum. That's why I didn't know what else to say. That's why I laughed."

"So this is a joke to you?"

"No," says Taft, staring down at his alarmingly deformed cock. "Don't you want me to answer honestly? I honestly don't want to cum."

He thought he had explained to her previously that he liked prolonged arousal more than orgasm. Obviously it hadn't registered. Or maybe that had been when he was chatting online with the Speaker of the House's wife. He can't remember now.

"Take the rubber bands off." It is certainly the same tone of voice she uses to tell her daughter to put the cookie she swiped back into the cookie jar.

Getting them off is difficult, especially since he is panicked that his cock is hurt. There isn't much room to get a grip on them. Finally he does and discovers his cock is sticky.

Did he cum without knowing it? Or is this all precum squeezed out by the rubber bands? Though the question is fascinating to him, it is of absolutely no interest to her.

"I don't like to be made fun of," she says, and hangs up.

He goes into the bathroom for an inspection. There are a couple red marks on his shaft, abrasions. He hopes they will disappear, in time.

And he makes a presidential decision. *I don't want a domme with no sense of humor.*

Michelle is obviously more rigid than his cock.

And there is no place for rigidity in politics. Principles are fine—as long as they are flexible.

HARPER

Your life—all the important stuff—is supposed to flash before your eyes. But instead, I'm dwelling on the ontological import of a semantic disagreement: should you tell a domme what she wants to hear or be honest about your orgasm denial fetish?

I feel like I am having an unending wet dream—like I'm a teenager again, but with a dirty old man's mind. Cumming and going at the same time.

PUBLISHER'S NOTE

This might help you understand what you have been reading up until now, if for some unfathomable reason you have stayed with this so far:

Youth was wasted on the young Harper Moross. He was painfully shy, and even when he went on a date and the girl obviously liked him, he had no idea what to do.

It took him a long time to get over being raised Catholic. He was ashamed of himself and painfully shy. Just when he started to think that perhaps his thoughts were wonderful rather than impure, he was smacked in the face by feminism, 1970s style. *All men are rapists!* He soon became so apologetic for having a penis at all that eventually he withdrew from dating and marrying women altogether. If women were not going to shave their legs and armpits and not wear makeup, why not just be with men?

You're born gay or you're recruited—those are the two prevalent views. Harper was neither. He became gay out of sheer boredom at being a Sensitive Feminist Man. It didn't do him much good to be a SFM, because even SFM still had penises and thus were potential rapists to be hated by feminist women, and he wasn't enough of a jerk to attract the women who had sex only with jerks. So he turned to men as a strategic move.

But that didn't work either, because he wasn't gay, just a failure at being straight.

So he was left, as he lay dying, with a lot of ridiculous unfulfilled fantasies. Excuse us for including them. But at this publishing house, we are dedicated to teasing out the truth, no matter how painful it is. We understand the difference between memoir, fiction, and nonfiction, and we are making absolutely certain that you understand it too.

HAL AND VERA

It's the long night of the viral payback. Son and daughter call Vera and Hal from California and Hong Kong. Other relatives and friends ring in between endless media requests for interviews.

That's how they find out about the video that the whole world is watching. The video of Vera going down on Harper.

So they watch it too. At first Hal is distracted. He's still trying to figure out whether that Marcuse scholar swiped his wallet while she was desublimating his repression. Then Hal sees, for the first time in his life, another man's cock in Vera's mouth. He doesn't tell her how much this arouses him.

"Why in the world would you videotape this?" asks Hal, but his voice is more wondering than accusatory.

"I didn't," she says, weepy.

"Then who did? It's actually…" Hal stops himself before he says "really fucking hot."

Vera suddenly puts it all together.

"It's the Home Cam."

"The what?"

"We started putting up Virtual Tours, like everyone else. Then when the market got *really* tight, on some of our bigger properties we installed cams to broadcast continually in some of the better rooms. This one was actually the Chases' idea—to put it in the kitchen."

"In case a dinner just happened to start cooking itself on the stove?"

"I suppose."

"But why would someone put this on?"

Vera ponders as Hal's mouth drops at the sight of Vera's lips engulfing the head of Harper's cock. *When did she learn how to do that?*

"Shit!"

Daniella. *Of course.* Demoted from junior agent to office manager because of the downturn. Has had it in for Vera ever since Vera complained to the boss that Daniella was crowding in on her territory, and word got back to the little bitch. Of late she's been failing to pass along phone messages and otherwise trying to screw up Vera's business.

"Damn," cries Vera. "I can't ever go back to work there again. Oh fuck, Hal, we're screwed. I'm so sorry."

But instead of slapping her like she deserves, Hal gives her a big hug and over his shoulder watches, rapt, as Vera takes all of Harper's cock in her mouth. Then he *does* feel like slapping her—but for a different reason.

"Jesus, Hal, why aren't you yelling at me?"

He bites his lip, then blurts out something he can't believe he's saying: "Actually, Vera, maybe we can make some money off this."

FOX 2 NEWS

At 4 a.m. the night nurse on duty at the main desk in the Surgical ICU is bored. Sitting at her station, she is fingering her PDA—looking at a bondage web site that features girls in medical scenes.

Seb Harpo, ace reporter, has no trouble sneaking by her despite his flaming hair.

Harper Moross is hooked up to so many tubes that he looks like the guinea pig in a mad scientist's experiment.

The sheet over his body is a huge tent.

The Reporter investigates. After all, he is an experienced investigative reporter. So he knows some very sophisticated techniques.

Like lifting up a sheet to peer under it.

LOIS

I'm skipping through a field of flowers. I'm *so* cute. I'm wearing my favorite Gothic Lolita outfit: white stockings speckled with little pink roses, a white flouncy dress with two frilly slips underneath it, a parasol, and a backpack with a Hello Kitty doll. I'm giddily soaking up the kisses of the warm sun.

Suddenly I notice I've snagged my stockings. Why is there a thorn in the midst of this field of daisies?

A shriek.

Is it my own voice?

No. It's Miranda's. Her squeal pulls me out of my dream.

"Lo, you gotta see this!"

I wince and squint at the clock. Six fucking thirty in the fucking morning.

"*Lois* Mayne! Are you *still* asleep?"

The price for getting to be submissive in bed is steep: enduring demands like these from the Witch Queen. How does Miranda Mayhem purport to be such a sex-positive feminist yet fail to understand that dommes who presume they can boss around their subs outside of playtime are reenacting the tropes of patriarchal conjugal subjugation?

I gather up my long, tangled, dark-brown hair that's fallen around my creamy neck and luscious breasts and throw it behind me a tad dramatically, like Rapunzel tossing her hair rope from the window. I pad into the kitchen, where perky little Miranda is sitting as usual in front of her laptop, black-rimmed nerd glasses slipping down as usual across her tiny nose, page-boy haircut of blonde with magenta and green streaks with the perfect bangs already brushed into place *as usual*, wearing shorts and a wife-beater endearingly covered by a red mesh top. One look and I melt. You simply can't be mad at this girl for long! I hug her around the neck.

"What's so urgent, Mir?"

Miranda gestures toward the screen, on which is playing a grainy film of an old black woman going down on a dumpy old white man in a sparkling, empty kitchen.

"Look at that technique!" shouts Miranda.

"What about it? Looks pretty ordinary to me."

"See that? *There?* Look at the expression on her face! There is something about the way she sucks balls that totally shouts *Revolution! Power to the People!*"

I nod, pretending to understand.

"Plus, she's a *sista!* And she's sucking off a white guy. And take a look at how hard his cock is! Instant mass-audience identification! We can definitely use her!"

"But who is she?"

"Some Realtor in Michigan. There's already a gazillion blog posts about this. Look how many hits on the video."

"Ninety-seven hundred thousand? That's not so many."

"In twelve hours? That's some serious O Energy! No wonder the world seems brighter this morning—this video alone has got to be generating tons more orgone!"

Miranda's eyes tear up. I know what's she's thinking about—the afternoon in the woods in Maine, and the confessional-shaped box in the old living room. The hours that changed their life forever—and that soon will save the world, or so my wife says.

Truthfully, the tentative morning light looks as dim as ever to me, but I've learned not to question Miranda's most cherished fantasies. Because that way I get to enjoy some of *my* most cherished fantasies.

FOX 2 NEWS

When Seb Harpo walks into Mackenie Krieg's office without knocking, she looks up with sizzling anger.

"What the hell?"

"I have your follow-up."

"And?"

"Let's just say there will be lots of Depends sold after the noon news."

MIRANDA

"You're nuts."

Lois can be *so* bratty sometimes. She's watching me hurriedly but efficiently packing my suitcase and camera bag—and impudently questioning my judgment. I try to use my tolerant voice, but it's hard not to sound scolding when she's acting like this.

"We have to get to her before anyone else, that's all that matters. There'll be lots of offers for story rights. Now get dressed immediately, so you can drive me to the airport."

"I'm really tired of you ordering me around like…"

"Like what? Like you're my sub? Lois, dear, that's what a sub is supposed to do, follow orders."

"You're confusing playtime with work time again. Right now I'm your business partner, and I'm telling you this is a stupid squandering of scarce resources."

I put my hands on my hips and dish Lois my most impatient stare.

"This is not about the business per se. The business is just a way to raise funds and awareness. This is about the Revolution. Don't you understand that, after all these years?"

"Of course I do."

"Everything up until now was preparation for this moment. This is the moment we've been waiting for."

"Why? Because you liked the way that chick sucked that dude's cock?"

"Yes—in fact I did. But the bigger point is that a million people are watching. And then…hey wait! Look at this."

On my laptop, there's a live video feed of Fox 2 News from Detroit. An impossibly young-looking blonde is sitting behind the anchor desk, feigning a look of gravitas that's undermined by her provocative cleavage.

"Now here's the latest incredible development in the story we broke for you last night, of the encounter between the Real Estate Lady and the Pickle Heir. Here's Seb Harpo, live from Cottage Hospital."

Man with hair on fire.

"Thanks, Angie. Pickle magnate Harper Moross remains in critical condition, hanging between life and death. But in a Fox 2 News exclusive, we can report to you that there's one part of his anatomy that remains quite alive—and rather impressively so."

"Can you clarify this for our viewers?"

"Well, you may want to grab the remote if there are children in the room, because what I am about to reveal may be shocking. I have now witnessed myself that the warnings on Viagra commercials aren't baseless.

But this time we may have a new world's record—if Guiness tracks such things. At least twelve hours after his encounter with Vera McNamara, Harper Moross still was rigid with pleasure."

"And what about currently?" Angie's smile is ridiculously salacious.

"I just talked to an orderly on the unit, and she confirms that doctors have been able to bring the patient's blood pressure and heart rate down, but there's one thing that nobody can bring down…his manhood."

Lois bends down and hugs me.

"I'm getting dressed," she coos. "I'm coming with you."

"Good girl."

And for once I'm not saying that phrase just to get her to make me cum. This time I really mean it.

FOX 2 NEWS

Within an hour after Harpo breaks his astounding news to a breathless world, a small group of men begin milling in front of the hospital entrance. Two of them hoist a banner: *Men Against Pornography.*

A few more men arrive with signs:

PORN BRAINWASHES MEN
REAL MEN ARE NOT PORN STUDS
MEN ARE MORE THAN COCKS

The men attract a gawking crowd of passersby. Soon reporters returning from lunch emerge, along with their camera operators, from the ever-growing city of TV trucks in the parking lot across from Cottage Hospital.

As they hold up their microphones to catch the demonstrators, one man steps forward. He's a bearded ex-hippie mountain man trying hard to look respectable in an ill-fitting business suit. He holds up a book titled *Men Confront Pornography* and starts reading from it.

"While pornography promotes a male fantasy of continued societal power, its effect is to render men more powerless to meet their emotional needs."

"Is this a religious protest?" shouts a reporter.

The man ignores the question and continues to read:

"Substituting a supervised, manipulated, pseudo-sexual experience for the real enjoyment of sex is porn's way of co-opting sexual liberation."

"Who's paying you?" shouts Seb Harpo.

Joseph Maxwell looks keenly into the camera lenses.

"No one's paying me, but we're all paying a price. Every time we mistake a cum shot for freedom of expression, our humanity is diminished. Men and women are now actively participating, day by day, in their own degradation. Not to mention that constantly being titillated is a distraction from important issues, like poverty and climate change."

"How is Harper Moross being exploited? He's dying in there."

"His cock is not the sum of who Harper Moross is. That's how."

Inside Fox 2 News studios, a young intern at the control desk looks up at his supervisor.

"Don't we have to bleep out *cock?*"

"Hardly," barks Mackenzie Krieg. "It's a male rooster."

FLY ON THE WALL (D.C.)

(Fly on the Wall is a registered trademark of Cyborg Insects International Corp.)

"We're not as far ahead in the polls as we should be."

Mark Potts projects his customary persona of harboring intense concern but remaining in control. As a campaign strategist, it's a technique he has honed perfectly. He needs to be needed, so there's always a crisis he's selling, but he's also hawking the fact that he's the one to quell it.

The others in the conference room—young woman with a nose stud, older woman with long gray hair, geeky young guy with glasses and a pocket protector in his checked shirt, token Hispanic—all nod in agreement, because it is their job to do so.

"We've had slippage among older working-class women again. And even a few others are starting to see our opponent, that dinosaur, as a kind grandfatherly type."

The geek raises his hand.

"Yes, Phillips?"

"I've got the dossier you requested."

"Do tell us then," says Potts, swiveling around in his chair. No one else in the room has a chair that swivels. No one else has earned one.

"Former radical. Active in college with the Weather Underground. United Farm Workers in the '70s. Nuclear freeze in the early '80s. Antiwar but not affiliated, Cindy Sheehan fan and Code Pink member. Husband, college psych professor active in the party, donor, precinct delegate in '00 and '04 and '08.

"So," says Potts. "What we also know is that she can be very persuasive with older folks. Her *sales record* proves that."

Girl With Nose Stud giggles. "Not to mention the pictorial evidence."

Potts waves a hand as if brushing aside a fly.

"Even the best woman can make an error in judgment. This is what this campaign is about—giving everyone a chance, or, if they need one, a second chance to help us make the change we need in Congress."

Potts rises from his chair.

"She's going to need some new options. Lord knows she'll be getting lots of offers. But if anyone can think of a way she can feel better about herself by serving her country, well, who could blame her for listening?"

Token Hispanic speaks up. "This reporter there, Harpo, he's secretly sympathetic. I've got an intermediary on the ground in Michigan."

Potts puts his hands over his ears.

"Damn earwax. Can't hear a thing you're saying." With that, he scoops up his papers, smiles as he looks at his minions, and hurriedly leaves the room. "I'm sure you will all exercise your best judgment," he says over his shoulder as he closes the door.

CINDY FROM NOWHERE OHIO

Hi all you pathetic guys and gals! I'm Cindy, a bisexual BBW Dominant female living in Nowhere, Ohio (you'll *never* find out where, so don't even try!). I get off on telling people what to do by email and IM and webcam. No money exchanged, I'm not a pro, I do this for fun (that's *my* fun, not yours—lol). If I select you as one of my stable of subs, I'll domme you whenever I feel like. I give rewards to guys and girls who obey. Rewards could include pics of me, more webcam time, and maybe even some phone domming. I may even send you my panties to sniff if you really behave and eat all your vegetables. My favorite is I like to play the "Lolita" type babysitter. If you are really lucky I may cam with you an entire evening and act as your mean but sexy and flirty babysitter. I like to humiliate. I like to control some of your daily activities. I may tell you what your bedtime is and what you will wear to bed. I may give you corner time. I might have you guys wear panties on cam for me. If you disobey you will get punished. I won't let you eat your favorite food or I'll make you sleep in the bathtub. Maybe I'll ignore you for a few weeks. Disobey too much and no more webcam for you! I may make you run errands for me and buy little cheap things to show me on cam. On the cam I will tease you and make you do all kinds of things. I like to make guys sit in front of the cam with an uncooked egg in their mouth while I give them their next orders. You won't be able to speak and if you are not careful you'll break the egg and lose your webcam privileges. I am in full control. You have NO power. ***Listen carefully*** If you message me you must send a picture of yourself SUCKING YOUR THUMB. I know some of you don't like this idea but I don't care. You want to be my webcam sub then you'll do as I say. Tell me what day of the week I would have you for my complete control. I may want to give you a list of orders for the day. I get off knowing that all my subs are simultaneously sitting in their bathtubs from 7-8 p.m. sucking their thumbs while wearing only panties because I told them to. I will make you send a picture with some kind of time stamp to prove you obeyed me. When you message don't forget the thumb sucking picture or you have no chance.

DR. MORRIS

"I've never seen a case quite like this. That's why we've called you in."

I nod at this yokel's statement of the obvious while looking over the EKGs. My eyes struggle to focus. It was an awfully bumpy ride in from New York. Well worth the trouble, of course, given my hefty hourly consultant fee. And since this case has aroused national attention, it's going to vastly increase my notoriety, and you certainly can't put a price tag on *that*.

"There's plenty of activity in his pleasure centers, that's clear." I feel it adds to others' comfort levels if I start off simple.

"Hence his physical response."

What *is* this local doc's name again? I've already forgotten. Oh, well—continue on.

"All this activity is actually inhibiting the blood flow to the rest of his brain, so we need to break the connection by desensitizing the cerebral cortex to erotic thoughts. This man's mental strategy, his response to trauma, is to flood himself with pleasure."

"And how do we break the connection?"

"The problem is that because the heart attack occurred while his penis was erect, his brain is stuck in memory of sexual activity. Thus the pathways that might allow the penis to detumesce are destroyed, and his ability to think of anything else is blocked. So we have to ask: What might get him to stop thinking about sex?"

"Something terrifying?"

I wish I could remember the guy's name. Is it Dick? It couldn't be, could it?

"I treated a case similar to this one once—a case of uncontrollable tumescence. We tried all the counter-medications to the ED drugs, nothing worked. We need something to distract him."

"What would that be?"

"We can start with violent images. They usually break down resistance. Then we try to fish something out of his own memory that will cause him to lose his arousal."

I'm certainly not going to tell this Dick *exactly* how I do this. That would be like John Grishman revealing his storytelling secrets to some punk police detective who thinks he's a writer.

LOIS

I'm *so* freaked flying in thunderstorms. And this is the worst flight *ever*. When we get close to Chicago there's so much turbulence that I'm walking back from the toilet and I'm thrown right into this guy's lap. Guy is delighted of course, but he's so old and smells of Cheetos and his beard is so long and stinky and his hands on me are so creepy that I feel like I'm about to get finger-fucked by Moses. Then they announce we can't land at O'Hare until the storm moves through, and we circle for an extra *hour*. All this time with horribly vivid flashes of lightning. *We're all going to be electrocuted.* I grip Miranda's hand tightly and wish, as I often do in these situations, that my protector's hand were twice the size of mine rather than half. It's crowded and cramped, and there is nothing to eat. They even charge for water on Rip-off Airlines!

With the orgone accumulator under the seat in front of me, I have no place to put my legs. It's cold up in these storm clouds, and my legs are speckled with goose bumps. Miranda *insisted* I wear a short skirt—and, of course, she gets to choose my clothes when we travel. Miranda's more sensibly clad legs barely reach the floor, so why can't the box be under the seat in front of *her*? Because she always has to be the boss. At the moment I wish she were more like a mommy. I'm almost hyperventilating, but she's paying no attention to *me*. She's writing some kind of contract on her laptop. I *swear*, sometimes I think Miranda loves her MacBook Pro more than she loves me.

When we finally land, it only gets worse. The flight to Detroit is delayed by the same bad weather moving east. So many people are stranded that we can find only one seat in the concourse, and guess who has to curl up on the floor?

On a TV monitor above where we sit, *Hardball* is blaring.

"So what is it about this video of—well, there is no way to put this delicately—a rather garden-variety sex act—what about it has captured the attention of millions of online viewers? Is this simply the sign of the Dog Days of a congressional campaign that's become repetitive and tedious? That we're even here discussing this is testament to that." Chris Matthew's boyish face looks like it is about to melt from sheer boredom.

"To join us to discuss the Pickle Man's pickle is a panel. ..."

I nudge Miranda, who is still furiously typing on her laptop, and point to the TV.

"...This shows how sick our culture has become, thanks to Hollywood and the TV networks—all the purveyors of filth." The well-known, always-enraged

Soldier of Christ is spewing his usual venom. "And what's really sick about this is the part of the video where his eyes roll back in their sockets. That's what getting so many people watching—"

"It's also about the total degradation of a woman." It's the gray-haired Feminist Elder talking now. "Even after all these years, even after the historic political candidacies we have witnessed recently, women are still treated in our culture as pieces of meat."

Mathews interrupts. "But this woman is certainly voluntarily taking part. In fact, not to be too crude about it, but who is the meat here?"

"What does it matter?" The short-haired, pit bull Younger Feminist goes on the attack. "If women's liberation wasn't about freeing women to be as sexual as they want, as sexual as men have *always* gotten to be, what's the point?"

As if on cue, the three guests and the host all start interrupting and talking over one another. Matthews shouts the loudest.

"Let's get our guest in on this," he bellows, calling off the dogs. "Joseph Maxwell is with the group Men Against Pornography, and he's coming to us from our affiliate in Detroit, where he's been picketing all day with a group of men for—for what, Joseph? Why exactly are you upset?"

Maxwell, in a Detroit TV studio, looks a bit sweaty and constrained in his sports jacket.

"Who says this is liberation for men *or* women?" he ventures. "I mean, Harper Moross didn't know he was being videotaped. He didn't know he was being exploited for a porn film that would be broadcast worldwide. He is being humiliated while he is dying."

Miranda jumps out of her chair and shakes her fist at the screen.

"Why the hell aren't we on there?" she shouts, as everyone in the whole fucking airport stares at her. "Nobody's speaking up for the awesome power of orgone!"

NURSE'S REPORT

11:20 p.m. Patient is unconscious, but his eyes are open and he appears to be watching the television. Patient has his thumb in his mouth and is sucking it. Check his vitals (no change). I ask him if he wants anything, not expecting an answer, because he has made no verbal contact since he was admitted. But then I hear him mutter one word, over and over, without taking his thumb out of his mouth. It sounds like "Cindy."

HARPER

The newspaper and TV images of atrocities that have always been in the background of my life are now in the foreground.

The photo of the naked Vietnamese girl running screaming through the bloody remains of her burning village—the one that appeared in all the newspapers—has come to life. And I'm *there*. I'm watching the American soldiers poke their bayonets into the breasts of young women, whose little children are clinging to their skirts crying. I try to avert my eyes, but I can't. I watch in horror as the soldiers rape the women, throw them into a ditch, and then spray the women and children with rifle fire. Some of the kids run off screaming into the jungle; others wail in their dying mothers' arms.

I watch in horror as napalm rains down on the perimeter of the village, where the elderly and infirm cannot escape the fire from the sky.

It's *A Clockwork Orange*—but with *me* strapped in the chair, my eyelids taped open, helplessly being forced to see all the carnage close up.

Videos from the jihad. A Western taken hostage, on his knees, mouthing praise to Allah, begging for mercy. The sword passing cleanly through his neck, slicing from one shoulder to the other, severing his head, until it drops to the ground like a pumpkin tumbling off a lamppost. *It is so easy to dismember a human being.* The head held up by the scalp, triumphantly. *We're always so totally vulnerable to each other. We prey on ourselves.*

Images from the war just before I was conceived: Gaunt ghosts thrown onto train cars, headed toward the concentration camps. A few broken survivors in Hiroshima, mere shadows of human beings, crawling through the rubble where a few minutes ago a city bustled. Stalin's pogroms, dissenters freezing to death on the Siberian steppes. And forward and backward through my lifetime: Pol Pot's genocidal madness, Pinochet's brutal tortures, men herded into a stadium then mowed down by rifle fire, El Salvador, Nicaragua, Rwanda, Darfur....

This is my so-called life—that is, the life and death of others witnessed by me from afar—but I'm now immersed in it, close up. Of course I can't stop it. I can only watch in horror as human beings murder millions of other human beings, for pride, for sport, for nation, for religion, for false hope, for lies.

HAL

It's after midnight, but I can't sleep. Vera's gone to bed. She must have taken a sleeping pill, because she's not tossing and turning like usual; she's lying still.

I turn on the TV. There's a breaking news bulletin: ISRAEL INVADES SOUTHERN LEBANON. Men, women, and children are throwing rocks and Molotov cocktails at tanks that are rolling over their homes.

I turn it off.

I peel off my clothes, walk out on the deck, and climb into the hot tub. There's no moon, and it's so dark I can barely see the shed in the backyard. Our black cat climbs onto the edge of the tub. I squint to see the stars through the light pollution, but all I can see is my wife's mouth around that guy's cock.

Barack starts to bark frantically.

Someone at the door! I climb out of the tub, run into the bathroom, towel off as best as I can, and pull on a powder-blue pool robe. Vera doesn't stir in the bed even though Barack is going nuts. I'm dripping as I plod down the stairs.

When I open the door, I think: I must be dreaming. There's a tall dark-haired beauty in a short leather skirt, boots, and shocking stockings. Holding her hand is a short cute geeky blonde in a sassy hat, sexy glasses, fashionable business suit, and lace-up fuck-me shoes. Barack immediately jumps up to sniff both of these interesting new crotches, and I notice he has an erection.

"Sorry, don't mind him."

"Oh, he's *so* cute," coos the short one. The tall one looks disgusted.

"I'm Miranda Mayhem, and this is my, um, *assistant,* Lois Mayne, and we have an offer for you. I hope it's not too late."

Too late? I'm naked underneath my pool robe, my wife has taken a sleeping pill and is out for the night, two gorgeous vixens are on my doorstep, and they want to make me an offer?

"Not too late at all. Come on in. I like staying up late."

Boy, do I ever!

ANGEL OF MERCY

It's late. Outside the hospital, yawning technicians and burned-out reporters keep going on coffee, small talk, and video games. Finally, the media crowd starts to thin.

No one notices when the strange-looking woman in the mad outfit cruises past the doors, blitzes around the nurse's station, and takes a seat beside Harper's bed. He is quiet; only the machines beep for him.

I look under the bed sheet.

I check the monitors.

I do the best thing for everyone.

HARPER (GOING)

"Home Depot," she says cheerily, holding up a couple of metal clasps. "It's the best place for buying stuff." She pulls out a chain and more pieces of hardware from her bag.

Her toy bag is like one of those comic magician's props. There's so much stuff in it there must be a hole in the bottom. She keeps yanking things out of it—dildos, leashes, vibrators, gags, blindfolds, hardware, pieces of ropes, inscrutable devices—putting them on the bed, and commenting on many of them. "I have this black collar," she says. "But I like this little white one better." "Damn, where's my butt plug?" "Shit, where's the batteries for this thing?"

Finally, she manages to select a collar and leash, and I put them on and tell her to crawl on the floor. I know that's the kind of thing that a dom is supposed to make a sub do. But I'm not sure what to do next. She looks up at me and laughs: "You're trying to be a serious dom. But then you break out in a big smile."

That's how it begins: My enchanted playground time with Meg. She's a big woman with a generous heart and an evil mind and *lots* of experience with BDSM. She's so matter-of-fact and curious and playful that we're like two little kids playing doctor. She's patient with me. She knows I'm not really a dom, just pretending to be one, so she helps me along. She likes my imagination, and she likes my tongue. We try stuff I've never done and, even more amazingly, a few things *she's* never done—despite the depth of her toy bag.

Finally, after all these years, I'm letting my mind run free. I've got someone who is eager to try anything I propose. I don't care if it's all in my head. It *feels* so real.

Meg is bisexual, of course—isn't every girl these days? She's also a "switch," and she's moving out of town. When she tells me how much fun she had domming another guy's wife, I decide to give her a parting gift that I'll enjoy too.

If live is a labor of love, I'll slave forever.

The words are tattooed on Cayenne's upper back.

Cayenne is even younger than Meg but no less experienced as a submissive. She's a wise-ass but strangely captivating. She's also half-blind and is missing part of her brain through some kind of birth defect, though you'd never know it from the sharpness of her wit and conversation.

We meet for lunch, and she tells me a long story about going to some party and being tied up and having a TENS unit used on her, even though she's afraid of electricity. I have no idea what she's talking about.

"I have to *tell* you," she confides. "I was just chatting with this guy online, and he wanted me to put canned fruit in my pussy and then fuck me."

"Well, did you?"

"I'll do anything once."

Cayenne has another dom who recently stuffed her in the trunk of his car and took her for a ride. Next, he wants to tie her to some railroad tracks.

She's willing to do anything. What more could you ask for in a going-away Gift?

At the Motel 6, where they leave the light on for you, the three of us meet. Meg leashes up the Gift, ties her onto the bed, and starts flogging her back and ass. She does so with extreme relish. I watch in amazement, and sometimes try to join in, but I don't want to step on her toes. Meg is totally concentrated on the Gift. Every so often she stops flogging her and does other things, whispering in her ear, slicing at her nipple with an ice cube, and dropping candle wax onto her breasts, stomach, and pussy. But the flogging always resumes. Soon she turns the Gift over on her back, and the blows rain down on her breasts.

After awhile Meg asks the Gift how much pain she is feeling on a scale of 1 to 10. Cayenne replies in a husky whisper, "Two." I gulp. Meg is spurred on to more violent blows. She slashes away at the Gift's breast, stomach, thighs. Cayenne's beautiful little breasts grow bruised and pulpy. I feel nauseous. Then Meg puts a vibrator into the Gift's pussy and flogs away. On and on and on and on. Finally Meg orders the Gift to masturbate and flogs her breasts repeatedly.

"When you cum, I'll stop hitting you," she says sternly. It seems to me to take forever, and then finally the vibrator pops out of her pussy and she rolls over onto her side, exhausted.

"Did she cum?" Meg asks me. She asks *me?*

The scene plays over and over in my brain, and each time it's replayed it becomes more like a horror movie. I do nothing while I watch the woman I trust raise her whip again and again and land it on the body of the woman I am supposed to be protecting. The Gift never complains. Finally, in mid-frame I scream:

"Meg, stop! Stop hitting her!"

I yell the words but cannot hear them.

She does not stop. I cannot stop her.

I, the helpless Watcher, become the Gift and curl up on the bed in a fetal position.

Did she cum? Did I cum?

I don't know. I know nothing any more. My mind is finally, blessedly, empty.

FOX 2 NEWS

The sun has barely broken the horizon when Dr. Morris and Dr. Dick emerge from behind the heavy old oaken front doors and onto the front steps of the century-old hospital. Sleepy reporters are still hastily applying touches of makeup as they yank microphones into the physicians' faces.

Dr. Dick clears his throat. "We're here to report the latest on the condition of Harper Moross. I'm afraid that despite all our efforts, the patient is being kept alive now only by machine."

Reporters shout questions. Morris steps up to bat.

"We tried the most promising methods of decoupling his consciousness from his arousal and thereby trying to pull him out of his comatose state," says the renowned doctor from the East Coast. "But his brain function had deteriorated too thoroughly. And now his brain is not functioning at all."

"What do you mean?"

"To speak plainly, Harper Moross is brain dead."

XIX'S FACEBOOK WALL

Angel report: We don't need no more fucking pretense or illusion. We don't need no shit-faced hypocrisy about morality. Human beings have always fucked each other, fucked with each other, and fucked up each other, and now they have fucked up the planet too.

Rise up and slap those pricks. Fuck 'em good and slap 'em hard, take everything they got and leave 'em begging for more of that rough treatment they so ardently desire and so richly deserve.

We don't need no more instruction. We don't need no more distraction. What we need is a wakeup call. What we need is a martyr.

And now we got one.

HARPER MOROSS'S OBITUARY

The last heir of a declining pickle manufacturing fortune is dead at the age of sixty

Harper Sebastian Moross, chief executive officer of the Seven Mile Pickle Corporation, maker of Splvasic Pickles, succumbed due to complications from a heart attack he suffered while getting his first decent blow job in twenty years.

Subsequent to his death, Moross, who had a history of chronic erectile dysfunction, had sustained what most experts say was the longest continuous erection in the history of the world—while in a coma.

It was the crowning achievement of Moross's controversial career as a pervert, which began with charting nylons in eighth grade and included several stints as a cuckold, a brief fling with bisexuality, and a short tenure as a freelance reviewer of fetish web sites.

At the time of his death Moross was reportedly working on a salacious autobiography that would "set the record straight," according to a woman who claimed to be his literary agent.

OFFICER H.M
SEBASTIAN

I *hate* kowtowing to the prosecutor. I won't even need this slimy job after my book becomes a best-seller. But since this ridiculous sleazy affair has become so high profile, it's smart politics to deliver my report directly to the Boss. And nobody in this whole department is smarter than I am.

My boss is Morgan Freeman. Or will be played by Morgan Freedom in the movie version of this book. He is gruff, wise, tough, tender, and omniscient.

I hand the printout of my report to the Prosecutor. The prosecutor devours it voraciously. *No trauma to the body. Suspect is cooperative, remorseful, ashamed, but insists she did nothing untoward. No apparent motivation on her part to do harm. A simple tryst, tawdry but otherwise harmless.*

Prosecutor Freeman looks up.

"And what about the videotape?"

I try not to look as smug as I feel.

"I looked into that. The camera was constantly running. It was part of their sales pitch on the real estate agency website, to show the updated kitchen. The suspect thinks someone in the office who is jealous of her success is the one who put the video up. If you want, I could investigate that aspect further but…"

"No need," says Morgan Freeman, in his most soothing Almighty tone. "You've done a fine job. Not everything in this world is knowable, and we can't judge other people's morality. That's not what the law is for. The law is a blunt instrument for protecting people from harm, and punishing those who do harm. But what is the harm in an apparently frustrated old woman trying to make the life of a lonely and apparently friendless old man a little brighter? And if her ministrations of mercy were too much for the poor man's heart, then how can she be held to blame? There are no charges to be brought in this case—and so I will bring this little circus to an end. Thank you, officer DeBanion."

"Thank you, sir. And it's Officer Sebastian."

But the prosecutor has already turned his attention to something on his computer screen.

Even God likes free porn.

DR. DICK

Miracle Man from New York is certainly full of excuses.

"I *told* you there was a risk to the sensual desensitization shock treatment."

"But you said the risk was minimal."

I'm really upset. Harper Moross is my patient, after all—that is, he's my patient if something goes terribly wrong, like this. If it goes right, then of course Mr. Harvard Medical School Hotshot is the savior.

"Minimal does not mean nonexistent."

My insurance premiums are just going to fucking *skyrocket,* that's for damned sure.

HARPER

It's murky on the bottom of the lake, so murky that if you sit, as I do, on the bottom of the lake for endless eons of time, your eyes still can never focus enough to see the hand in front of your face.

But now there is a shape off in the mist. A prehistoric fish? No. Two shapes, joined at the ends of their arms. As the shapes approach, the gloom seems to run away from their presence. They're shining with a bluish light that banishes darkness. The light of fresh, energized young women. It radiates from the tall one's delicious thighs, her radiant lips. It shoots up from the short one's shiny little shoes with straps and buckles, and it pulses from her neck and bare shoulders. It's a life-giving light.

Under the sheet the phallus that the whole world has seen begins to stir anew.

And when I completely wake up, it *is* just like being a kid again—my sheets are wet and sticky and have that strange yeasty metallic smell.

ALL NEWS OUTLETS EVERYWHERE

It's but a few moments until the news is on everyone's front page.

PICKLE MAN SPRINGS BACK TO LIFE
Medical miracle in Motown

As the news breaks, Joseph Maxwell and the Men Against Pornography are holding a press conference to express their outrage at the prosecutor's announcement that no charges will be brought against Vera McNamara.

"Harper Moross is the victim here!" insists Maxwell. "And so are all men who are being polluted by the constant stream of pornography flowing unimpeded across the Internet. Clever six-year-olds can find this stuff easily. What does it say to a young boy when he sees images like this? And yet no one is going to be charged because men are never seen as the ones who are exploited. A man is dead today because—"

One of the Men Against Pornography whispers hastily in Maxwell's ear.

"A man is alive today, barely alive, his reputation permanently damaged, and ready to be exploited again. Why isn't the prosecutor going after whoever it is that took and released this videotape? The public deserves to know! And until we do know, there will always be a suspicion—a suspicion about who was *really* behind this."

FOX 2 NEWS

Just the sight of Seb Harpo's lanky, lackadaisical stride as he approached her office used to make Mackenzie Krieg feel like growling. Now, it makes her feel a stirring in her loins—something she hasn't felt this entire millennium.

"I got the full story."

He's almost crowing, damn him.

"Just by sitting at your computer?"

"Got spies inside with cell phones. You ought to learn about text messages."

"I don't care what methods you use, as long as you make our audiences cum."

"Oh, they'll cum hard. Nothing like an orderly with a camera phone at the right time."

HARPER

I rip the tubes out of my body and walk on my own, feeling a bit wobbly but surefooted nonetheless, into the bathroom.

That's odd. Something on my stomach. A couple crosses connected by a line?

In black lipstick.

FOX 2 NEWS

The whole world is watching to see what's fair and accurate. They will learn it from the man with the flaming bush on his head.

"This is Seb Harpo, with an exclusive report from a firsthand witness to the remarkable resurrection of pickled poker Harper Moross."

He's sitting behind a desk with a video screen behind him.

"We have an exclusive video taken anonymously by someone with a camera phone."

The grainy images show Harper's hospital room.

"See, the patient is lying motionless, except for his chest heaving up and down as the ventilator forces him to breathe. There, you see two women approaching the bed. Then watch, something stirs under the sheets …"

The video suddenly has a bluish tint to it, like something has changed in the color processing.

"…something we've all grown accustomed to these last few days. And now you see his eyes pop open. And immediately he speaks…"

"Holy shit! I must have died and gone to heaven!"

The camera shifts from the video to a close-up of Harpo's face.

"And who are these angels of mercy who seemingly brought Harper Moross back to life? They're joining us now for an exclusive interview. Miranda Mayhem and Lois Mayne."

The camera pulls back to reveal the two young temptresses walking into the studio and taking seats in chairs beside Harpo. Miranda is dressed in a jumper and knee socks. She's like a parochial schoolgirl. And just as perky a proselytizer as a Jehovah's Witness.

"How do you explain what happened when you came into Harper Moross's room?" Harpo asks.

Miranda does all the talking.

"The power of sexual expression is unlimited and largely untapped. This incident proves that. The time for skepticism is over now. Wilhelm was right!"

"Whoa. Slow down now. Can you explain for our viewers?"

"Orgone is a gaseous, odorless substance, but it emits a color in the visible spectrum. Did you see the blue? That was solid evidence of the orgone emitted when Harper Moross had his orgasm, an orgasm so powerful it brought him back from the dead. And if orgone can do *that*, imagine what it can do as a source of alternative energy! No more climate crisis, no more dependence on foreign oil and fossil fuels."

"That's quite a leap, Ms. Mayhem. Are you saying it was your presence that awakened Harper Moross?"

Miranda and Lois both look into the camera directly, their lips parting just a little, lasciviously gazing at the throngs they intend to bring to their knees.

"My assistant Lo and I have trained for years at enhancing our capacity to produce orgone for the good of all humankind. Many people mistakenly believe orgasms are solely a physical phenomenon, when there is clear evidence they can be mentally induced. In fact, I'm quite confident that, just from our appearance on your show, the orgone level of the planet has increased significantly. And that is why the video of Harper Moross getting a blow job has been so beneficial to the health of the Earth."

"Do you mean ozone?"

"No, not *ozone*. *Orgone*. The substance discovered by the great psychologist, scientist, and philosopher Wilhelm Reich in his retreat in Maine in the 1940s. It's always been present in the universe, but the forces of repression keep trying to clamp down on it. That's why there are so many laws about who can fuck whom, and all this religious claptrap about marital fidelity, it's all designed to keep us from orgasming daily and thus freeing ourselves from the hegemony of the patriarchal corporate capitalist system…"

In the studio, Krieg slices her own throat with her finger. The "cut" sign has an immediate effect. The cameras return to the anchor desk in another studio, behind which sits a stern old veteran who ad-libs: "Thank you, Seb Harpo, for that fascinating exclusive."

Mackenzie Krieg shakes her head. "That woman was fucking nuts," she tells her technicians. "And to think I trusted Harpo to be something other than the clown he always is."

Then she notices the phones are ringing off the hook.

Highest ratings *ever!*

VERA

I'm nervous as hell. This is the first time I've been out of my house since I became a celebrity, and I'm scared to death someone will notice me. I'm hoping my old blond Tina Turner wig is a good disguise. I fished it out from the back of my closet with the other costumes I wore long ago when we used to go to Halloween parties. I'm using white makeup and trying to pass for white too. That's easy, I've done that many times.

The place I was told to come for the meeting is in a brand new strip mall way beyond the outskirts of town. I'm relieved that there are only a few cars in the parking lot. Besides the café, the only other place open here is a nail salon.

He's sitting in a corner booth, dressed like he said he'd be—in shorts and a Hawaiian shirt, a Panama hat and sunglasses. He looks like Jimmy Buffet.

As I get closer, I see he's also wearing a blond wig, rather sloppily.

"Funny," I quip, trying to play it cool. "You don't *look* like Deep Throat."

He shakes my outstretched hand.

"If you don't mind my saying so, neither do you."

I laugh. I like a guy with a ballsy sense of humor. And then I realize it's the first time I've laughed since before Harper Moross came down my throat.

We order our coffees and don't waste any time on small talk.

"I'm just a messenger," he says.

"I understand."

"You've become rather well known, so it's been easy for people to find out things about you. The people who I've been in contact with know about your history and your political leanings."

"Is that so?"

"Yes, and they also know that you're a patriot, and that you would be happy to do your share to help make history."

"In what way?"

"To be part of the change we need in Congress."

"Ahh. You mean the change we can believe in? *That* change?"

The man looks away, then makes a zipping-his-lip gesture.

"Certain skills of yours are, of course, rather well known. That makes you potentially a formidable weapon."

"Does it now?"

"Yes, in fact, in the opinion of some, your mere presence in certain situations could be inflammatory."

This is just making me more nervous. I'm not sure I like being some sort of heat-seeking missile. I swallow hard and persist.

"Say more, please."

I notice a curl of red hair protruding from the bottom of his blond wig.

"I can't say much more. I know you're not skilled at infiltration. But you do seem adept at disguises. And with a little bit of help that skill can get you past security and into the orbit of the candidate for Congress whose change we can't believe in. And once there, if you remove your wig and get in front of the cameras, well—that's all that will be necessary. Because the press can be manipulated from there."

"I *think* I'm following."

"If you will please excuse me, I have to go to the men's room."

He stands up, grabs his small satchel, and sets it down on the bench on his side of the booth. Then, instead of going to the bathroom, he heads out the door.

At first I wonder if I should grab the satchel and run after him, yelling, "Hey, you left this behind!" But I quickly come to my senses. I gather up the satchel and walk to my car as nonchalantly as I can, considering my heart is thumping halfway out of my chest. I drive down the road and spy a parking area for an old gravel pit. I stop, get out, look in all directions, then open the bag.

Inside is a detailed itinerary, an instruction sheet, and more cash than I've ever seen in my life.

HAL

I'm having lunch at my favorite Chinese restaurant with my new best friends, Mir and Lo. There are benefits.

"So you've actually read Reich?" asks Miranda, a chopstick lingering tantalizingly below her lower lip. There's something that looks like a chopstick in her hair too—it goes well with her flowered kimono and her bright red geisha mouth.

"Of course, I majored in psychology."

"But Reich isn't taught in most schools anymore."

"Well, he wasn't in my day either. But *The Mass Psychology of Fascism* was a popular book among radicals in the Vietnam era. We all thought it was brilliant. I gobbled up everything Reich wrote, including *The Function of the Orgasm*."

"And your conclusion? Was he a dangerous fraud touting unproven cures for cancer?"

"I think most cures for cancer are dangerous frauds."

Miranda twirls her chopstick in her lo mein, while Lo Mayne twirls a lock of Miranda's hair between her fingers.

"No wonder you're so easy to convince."

"You're very convincing."

"You see," says Miranda, waxing scholarly, "Einstein was wrong when he tested the orgone accumulator. He only measured temperature, but he should have been looking at other things—energy, shifts in the aura, things even he didn't fully understand at the time."

"So what do you say to the skeptics?"

"The evidence is right in front of your face. Orgone's blue. And the sky is getting bluer all the time."

"Some would say that's because the ozone layer is burning off."

"It has more to do with the orgone layer. It just so happens that the so-called depletion of the ozone follows a timeline very similar to the spread of the Internet and the availability of personal PCs."

"So?"

"So the cheap and easy availability of porn online, and how easy it's become meeting sex partners on the web, and the rise of Third Wave Feminism—they've all contributed to a rise in orgone levels."

"So if that's the case, why haven't we all been liberated yet?"

I ask this even though I'm feeling more liberated by the second.

"Not nearly enough orgone yet, of course. People are still locked up in shame and guilt. They don't cum nearly enough. And they don't understand that having an orgasm is not just a selfish thing. It's your contribution to the survival of the planet."

I'm liking this planet crisis more and more all the time Miranda keeps talking. I love how enthusiastic she is about her work.

"Reich's accumulator was the first step. We were there, Lo and I. We visited Orgonon, or what remained of it. We saw the accumulator in Reich's house. We sat inside it."

"How was that?" I ask. Lo winks at me. Miranda ignores her.

"We've discovered you don't really need to sit in a box to produce orgone. All you need to do is to have more and more orgasms, and then you release this literally life-saving substance into the atmosphere. It's the solution to the energy crisis, the solution to global warming, and the solution to all the violence and conflict and unhappiness on Earth. If everyone were having more orgasms, we'd be fighting one another a lot less."

I sit back in my chair and entwine my hands behind my neck. Could this really get any better? Unfortunately, my brain keeps analyzing.

"So why have you approached me?"

"I think you know why. We hinted at this last night. Your wife right now is the hottest orgone-stimulating property on the planet—well, next to the two of us, anyway."

At this Lois smiles coyly.

"But a lot of people, and—no offense intended—especially a lot of people your age, don't feel free to enjoy Vera's abilities because she's married. However— "

Miranda pushes forward a stapled set of papers.

"With this contract I've drawn up, you release your presumptive ownership rights in Vera's orgasms and agree to allow her to pursue orgone-inducing activities as she wants."

The paper's on the letterhead of the Orgone Liberation Front, and it's entitled "Release of Conjugal Exclusivity and Obligations."

I start to read the contract, under which I am going to grant the rest of the world the right to pursue orgasms with the active help of my wife.

"What's this about 'If the undersigned predeceases the releasee, it is presumed that all rights granted revert to the Orgone Liberation Front?'"

"It means if you die before Vera, we get the right to manage her orgasms," smiles Miranda.

"And what do I get out of this?" I can't help but ask. "I mean, besides doing the right thing for humankind and the planet and all that?"

Mir traces a finger along Lo's lips.

"I think you already know that, don't you, sir? Didn't we make it all very clear last night?"

I grab the pen Lo offers me.

"Oh yes. Quite clear."

I sign my name in a bold flourish.

HARPER

It worked for Jim Croce, it worked for Joplin, it worked for Hendrix, it worked for Hemingway. It's true: Dying is a great career move.

Dying and coming back to life—even better. Jesus! I had to drown my cell phone in the toilet so it would stop ringing. My email box is flooded with offers. *Penthouse*, *Maxim*, *Esquire*, *Rolling Stone*—they all want to do shoots of me with Vera, or with my choice of porn stars. I'm getting lots of endorsement offers. Do I want to be a spokesman for Viagra?

No, there's only one thing I want.

I have to escape for awhile. All the tests show I'm perfectly healthy, but I need a little physical therapy and rest and recuperation. My clever solution is to check into a nursing home under an assumed name.

I take my laptop and the audacity of hope. I use the webcam on it and take plenty of pictures of me sucking my thumb and send them off. But I never get a reply from Cindy from Nowhere, Ohio.

Down the hall is a partially paralyzed young man, a veteran of Iraq. One of his legs is amputated, and he has very limited use of his arms and hands.

This is my closest contact ever with the carnage of the rest of the world. But I no longer care about that stuff. I do wonder how the guy gets off, though.

That first evening I hear some moans from down the hall. I ask an orderly what the hell is happening. Every night, he tells me, the man is stripped down and he is sat up in bed. An occupational therapist helps him turn on his laptop computer and play a porn video. He masturbates. Then staffers come back in and clean him up.

The orderly says they do this for him because he has threatened to sue if the staff were to refuse to assist him in his pursuing his "right" to this "activity of daily living."

VERA

My instructions say I'm supposed to go to Gate 4 at the auto plant at 3 p.m. Apparently that's where the target is going to give a speech about some hydrogen technology tax incentive initiative or something.

I put my wig back on and hide myself under a big UAW jacket that a student once gave Hal in exchange for a passing grade. But of course I don't tell Hal where I'm going. I haven't seen much of him lately anyway.

When I get to the gate, there's a crowd of supporters, a counter-demonstration, and a shitload of media. I'm really nervous someone's going to blow my cover.

A security guard is supposed to slip me credentials so I can get through the gate. I walk up to a guard who looks promising, but suddenly I feel an arm grabbing me from behind around my shoulders. Then a hand pulls off my wig. I scream as the candidate walks right past me, in a clot of bodyguards, and everyone is snapping pictures.

FOX 2 NEWS

Against a backdrop of various photos of Vera in the vicinity of the candidate—some of which show them practically at arm's length away, and both of them looking startled—Seb Harpo intones for his audience:

"I have learned from trusted sources that Vera McNamara's appearance at Congressman Bangford's campaign stop this afternoon was in fact a political double-cross. McNamara, she of near-lethal-blow-job fame, told reporters at the scene that she was given instructions by an emissary from the Democrats to go to the security gate, where she would gain admittance and approach Bangford and blow him a kiss in an effort to make it look like she was his mistress. But *my* sources tell me that the whole thing was set up by the Republicans' dirty-tricks division to make this look like a Democratic entrapment plot gone badly awry—and that it was a GOP emissary who contacted McNamara in the first place."

FLY ON THE WALL
(D.C.)

In an office just inside the Beltway, a grim-faced man with a huge diamond ring on his finger curses as he watches the network feed of Harpo's report.

"That little turd!" he says to his mousy male secretary. "He was playing both sides!"

CASSIE'S TAVERN

In Cassie's Tavern, a dive in Detroit where the ceiling's so low you have to bend down to get through the door, the Chief Conspiracy Theorist shakes his head after watching the conclusion of Seb Harpo's report on Fox 2 News.

"Can you *believe* this *bullshit*? Haven't you guys seen the pictures?"

The guy on the barstool to his right laughs.

"You mean the one of Bangford with his dick in that black chick's mouth?"

The guy on the barstool to the CCT's left objects.

"Dude, are you kidding me? His face was just Photoshopped onto the face of that guy who croaked after he came. It's so obvious!"

"Hey, he didn't croak! He had the longest-lasting erection in the history of the world, gonna be in the Guinness Book of World Records. But he recovered."

"Oh, *sure* he recovered," says the Chief Conspiracy Theorist. "That's why you never see him anymore. The whole thing was faked."

"What exactly was faked?" asks a guy down the bar.

"His death and fucking resurrection! There *was* no Harper Moross. I mean, c'mon, when was the last time you even *saw* a fucking Splvastic Pickle? The guy never existed. It was all a cover-up to save Bangford's ass. He got caught with his zipper down, plain and simple."

A man down at the other end of the bar gets up.

"Bangford was never even in Detroit that day. He was giving a speech in the House!"

The Chief Conspiracy Theorist is unfazed.

"Sure, they had a guy that *looked* and *acted* like him in the House. They do that all the time. All the candidates have stand-ins."

"Oh, c'mon—you think the news is just a charade?"

"If our own government can crash planes into buildings and *pretend* that's what made them fall down, when the laws of physics say they couldn't possibly have collapsed from those impacts, you think they're not capable of producing two Billy Bangfords?"

Another quarter is heard from: "I hear the whole thing was set up by the Democrats. *They're* the ones who recruited that woman—hell, she used to be a fucking *Black Panther*—just to bring down a war hero...."

In the next room a band is setting up. It's a hardcore rock group. The guys have shaved heads and big tattooed arms and two groupies: a large woman with red lips wearing a schoolgirl outfit with white stockings, and a shorter but even larger woman with red hair, bright lips, fishnet stockings, a short skirt, and a black top across which is emblazoned the assertion:

I SWALLOW.

XIX'S FACEBOOK WALL

Elections are the porn of politics. Reducing all the variety of possible political action to the mindless, repetitive coupling of one prick from each "party" trying to compete to see who's the fucker and who gets fucked. And now, just like the actual porn online, it's a loop tape. There's never a break in the election season. As soon as one prick gets in, a new prick competition starts for the next fuckfest. Voting? Fuck! Voting is nothing but voyeurism for idiots.

HAL

Ignoring the snickers and the whispered comments as I walk to the auditorium stage—"Cocksucker's old man!" "His wife's the blow-job queen!"—Old Professor Hal Pasten turns his back to the class one more time. I lift my marker to the whiteboard and write on it:

POLYMORPHOUS PERVERSITY

"Who can tell me what that means?"

I turn around, but Xix has already pulled the bubblegum out of her mouth.

"Easy one, teach. It's Freud's term for all the non-standard versions of sex, for everything but heterosexual vaginal intercourse. Oral, anal, foot fetish, breast bondage, enemas, spanking, water sports, asphyxiation…"

Xix's list is drowned out in laughter.

"OK, Xix, we get the point," I say. "You don't have to go through the entire BDSM lexicon."

Amy raises her hand.

"Yes, Amy?"

"Professor Pasten, what mean beady esem?"

Now there's a roar of guffaws. I decide to go for the gold.

"Never mind, Amy. I'll tell you after class. Special instructional section."

Now there are whistles, hoots, and shouts: "You go, man!" "Dude!" "Professor!"

Amy looks confused, turns beet red, and sits down.

I smile and launch.

"Freud's theory is that children go through these stages as infants and toddlers. During breastfeeding we go through the oral stage. During toilet training we go through an anal stage."

"You mean, like playing with your poop?" shouts out a frat boy.

I ignore him, even though he's absolutely correct.

"But so-called 'normal' adults are supposed to get beyond all this and become practitioners of approved sex, which is heterosexual intercourse. In order to do this, Freud recognized, we have to submit to massive repression. That's because human beings are, like most animal species, naturally polymorphous perverse.

"Polymorphous, of course, means 'many forms.' In practice, the only thing that limits the many ways in which people play together is the human imagination.

"So there are many ways of being perverse, as Xix started to tick off for us. But let's ask—what does *perverse* actually mean?"

I make the mistake of pausing.

"Sticking your finger up a girl's ass!"

"Feeding your cum to your girl's girlfriend."

"Jenna Jameson getting DP'd!"

"Having your wife suck another guy!"

Ouch. Well, at least the class is *finally* having a discussion.

"OK!" I admonish. "Keep it in your pants!"

Applause and whistles.

"*Perverse* comes from two Latin words. *Vers,* the root word, means 'to turn.' And *per* means 'through.'

"So if we go by the definition, what we call a 'pervert' is someone who has 'turned' sexual expression all the way through, past its approved purpose and into the arena of unauthorized imagination.

"So what exactly is wrong with this? What's wrong with using our minds and bodies to seek connections with other people? To desire to be joined to another person is what makes us most human, isn't it?"

Xix jumps up out of her seat.

"Yeah, why is it such a fucking *big deal?* Playing, sexual expression, it's just amusing—and often ridiculous."

"So why is that a problem for society?"

She faces me and trains her formidable brain on the problem.

"Organized religion, in cahoots with government. The Church made it into a duty, a chore. *Procreation.* Sex—an obligation! The Church had to demonize sex and control it—to keep people from realizing that we're all creators. We can make life all by ourselves. We're all gods—and we don't need religion. So the Church turned our most divine and wonderful powers into evil instruments of the devil, to stomp out all the pleasure, because we're not supposed to have joy and ecstasy until *after* we die! What a farce!"

There are cheers for Xix, and she executes an elaborate bow.

Then, to my chagrin, she leaps onto the stage, rushes toward me, and plants a big fat kiss on my lips. The class howls.

A CORNER OF THE WORLD

On the television set inside the house by the lake is a commercial for hurricane relief. Gaunt, starving kids in Haiti are reaching through, or trying to climb over, a fence topped with barbed wire that separates them from a truck. From the truck bed, soldiers are unloading boxes of food and trying to fend off a mob.

The woman ignores what's on the TV. She's sitting on the edge of a chair, and her attention is focused on the computer in front of her. Plugged into it is a cord that disappears under her skirt. On the monitor is a man on a webcam. They're messaging, and he's working a control dial on his computer. His device controls the intensity of the vibrations of the dildo that's inside her pussy.

In the house next door another woman hears a train whistle. Without touching herself, she instantly orgasms. That's what she's been instructed to do by email by *her* dom: cum whenever she hears a train.

Across the street from the two houses is a Lover's Lane sex toy emporium. Inside a salesgirl is flashing her cleavage while showing a man the store's selection of paddles. He picks out one with little heart-shaped holes in it. Tomorrow is Sweetest Day, after all, and how better for Daddy to show his love than to leave little hearts on his Baby Girl's sweet ass?

The man glances out the showroom window and sees a boy riding his bicycle across the front yards of the two houses. The boy has a path he's worn in the grass. The boy calls it Lover's Lane.

THE MOVIE VERSION

Let's reshoot the scene, OK?

Let's get it right this time. On the money. One take.

Ready, Harper?

Vera, all set? Good girl!

Lights! Camera! Action!

And down she goes, up and down, and all around, her tongue like a whirling dervish, her mouth like a Sears Reliable Vacuum, her lips like suction devices.

But I remain.

Remain in Control.

I'm going to make porn history. I don't even have to touch myself.

As I start to twitch, I push her head off me. She obediently releases my cock and sticks out her tongue.

The world's most famous cock finally produces.

I cum all over her tongue and her mouth and her face, great gobs of goo rocketing, bombs bursting in air.

A banner unfurls:

MISSION ACCOMPLISHED

PUBLISHER'S OFFICE

The Publisher sighs. He picks up another letter from the pile atop his desk. A previously unpublished author, a police officer to boot, with a "radical political 1960s sci-fi revenge fantasy." He scans the opening paragraph—*four pages long and something to do with the power of the sun? H.M. Sebastian? Are you kidding me?*

He picks up another. Clever—paper-clipped to the pitch is a back cover mockup with endorsements.

"A highly comic sex romp!"

"Mental masturbation with a huge payoff!"

"A true-to-life fake memoir!"

He notices the name: Harper Moross.

The publisher buzzes in his assistant.

She appears, a newspaper in her hand.

"Miss Knight, Harper Moross—isn't he the guy who almost died from a blow job?"

"I don't know, sir. I don't follow the news."

In unconcealed exasperation—*why do I work for this idiot anyway?*—she tosses the newspaper on his desk and turns on her heels.

He glances up at the TV suspended from the ceiling, with the stock-market crawl along the bottom:

DOW DOWN 300.

Above the crawl is a political ad. A close-up of an old guy's face. He's gasping and looks ecstatic. Words flash in big pink letters across the screen:

SAFE
CHEAP
ORGANIC
ALTERNATIVE ENERGY

An incredibly luscious woman's voice begs:
"Vote OLF. Time has cum today."

A shot of a short woman with glasses, pixie hair, and her hand on a leash that's around the neck of a much taller woman wearing a red leather dress.

"I'm Miranda Mayhem. And I approve this message."

The publisher looks down at the newspaper. There's a huge headline: IRAN NUKE SHOWDOWN.

He shrugs at the paper, then buzzes his assistant again and shouts excitedly into the speaker phone:

"Miss Knight, get me Harper Moross."